MYSTIC
JIVE

HAND OF FATE - BOOK FOUR

MYSTIC JIVE

HAND OF FATE - BOOK FOUR

SHARON JOSS

AJA PUBLISHING
USA

Published 2016 by Aja Publishing
www.ajapublishing.wordpress.com

Book and cover design Copyright © 2016 by Aja Publishing
Cover art & design by Lou Harper
© Adrianhillman | Dreamstime.com - <a href=”https://www.dreams-time.com/stock-image-tree-roots-image6769651#res5911311”>Tree
With Roots Photo</a>
Heraldic Griffin Design Copyright © by Buch / Dreamstime

Sign up for my new release mailing list at: http://bit.ly/1UkJZTa
Your email will never be shared and you can unsubscribe at any time.

QUALITY CONTROL: We care about producing error-free books. If you find a typo or formatting problem, send a note to sharonjoss.author@gmail.com so that it may be corrected.

PRINTED IN THE UNITED STATES OF AMERICA

ISBN: 978-1-941544-35-8

CHAPTER 1

CHARLIE CRIMMER AND I stood outside the historic clapboard farmhouse in south Webster with a big 'For Sale' sign out front. The roof looked new, but the siding looked dingy and the porch sagged like a swaybacked mule. The place had been empty for years, and was in the process of being readied for sale. Charlie and I exchanged a nervous glance. Last week, he'd had fallen right through the rotted second step of a seemingly well-maintained Dutch Colonial.

"It doesn't look haunted," I said.

Charlie's dark eyes twinkled. "Ladies first."

"Chicken." The floorboards groaned beneath my feet, but held. "Come on, don't be such a baby." I pulled off my gloves and dialed the combination on the realtor's lock attached to the front door handle.

When Jillian Safford, a big-name realtor specializing in historical properties first approached me with the idea of psychic cleansing an old estate for one of her buyers, I thought she was kidding. But she said that being able to offer buyers the services of the Hand of Fate to clear the house of any negative karma or restless spirits before they bought was a real selling point.

And the five hundred bucks a pop she offered changed my mind. A win-win for everybody. And since my secondary source of income had died after Dave's Killer Burgers shut down, I needed the cash.

So did Charlie. We were partners on this. Actually, I'm more like the chauffer. Without him, there *is* no business.

A couple hundred years ago, Charlie was shaman of the local Senequois tribe. Now, he's one of Morta's psychopomps—he escorts souls of the recently deceased through a portal to the land of the dead.

There are only a dozen or so of these portals in the world, and one of them is right here in Shore Haven. It sits beneath the fun house at Heavenly Shores Amusement Park, and with the park shut down for the winter, Charlie's hours as a part-time security guard are cut to the bone.

Even the undead have to make a living.

A sudden gust of late September wind pelted us with fallen leaves, and I wished I'd worn something warmer than my leather jacket. The realtor lock clicked open and a big old brass skeleton key dropped into my palm. "Oh hey, check it out." I grinned and held it up for Charlie to get a look at. The key's filigreed handle was in the shape of a tree with a woody trunk for the shaft, and at the business end, a convoluted root ball.

"Hurry up, girlie." Charlie slapped his arms against the first bite of fall. "It's colder'n a witch's tit out here."

"Hang on." I slipped the heavy key into the lock. With a little jiggling, the tumblers engaged, and we were inside. A blast of chill air greeted us—it was like a refrigerator inside. Cold enough to see our breath, but at least we didn't have the wind.

We stood in the empty entry hall—parlor to the left, stairs straight ahead. There was just enough late afternoon light coming in from the windows to see our way around. Other than a sawhorse and a couple empty paint cans in the parlor, the immaculately restored interior looked move-in ready. The tang of fresh paint and pine-scented disinfectant choked the stale air.

Charlie hit the light switch, but nothing happened.

"Jillian thinks it's a poltergeist. It keeps smashing the light bulbs in their sockets. The workmen finally gave up and quit replacing them." My voice echoed across the bare floors in the empty house. Good thing we'd brought flashlights.

"Somethin' not right about this place," Charlie said. "Can you feel it?"

"There's a demon somewhere in the house," I answered. This was only the second time we'd come across a named djemon on one of our jobs. Over the last few months, my ability to sense djinn and djemons had gotten stronger. "In the basement, I think. Maybe that's it."

He shook his head. "Nope. Try again."

Usually I helped Charlie set up his smudge sticks and followed him around. He's got a real affinity for spirits and souls—some would call him a ghostmaster, but not in front of Charlie. He thinks that as I gain more of Morta's power, I'll be able to detect the presence of departed souls and spirits as well as he does. I closed my eyes and opened my senses to get a feel for the emotional tone of the place, like Charlie had taught me. Using a technique I'd learned from Master Foo, I took a deep cleansing breath and slowly exhaled.

Nothing. Nada. I'm not all that convinced I've got it in me.

Charlie led me to the stairs and placed my hand on the beautifully polished wood banister. "See if that works."

To my surprise, the crescent-shaped scar on the palm of my left hand buzzed like an angry bee. What the hell was that supposed to mean? "Hey," I pulled away, rubbing my hand on the back of my jeans. "What is that? Expectant? Nervous?"

He coughed. "Now you're just guessing." I knew he wanted a cigarette, but Jillian had forbidden him to smoke on the premises. Charlie went into the parlor and set down his nylon gym bag on the gleaming wood floors.

Annie, Charlie's djemon, materialized silently beside him. Annie's form is that of a pterodactyl.

I did a double-take when I got a look at her. I hadn't seen her for a while.

She'd been a sickly palm-sized kitten at the beginning of the summer. In the past four months, she'd grown into a pelican-sized bat-thing with a long, wicked-looking beak that would have given a heron pause. Her original master was dying when I found her. I'd given Annie to Charlie after I accidentally tore a hole in his soul. Banishing a demon can be tricky, and I'd used the wrong words when I'd banished his first djemon. Fortunately, Annie and Charlie had healed each other.

"Good night, how did she get so big?"

Charlie's usually grumpy expression melted away. He stroked the short black down on her head affectionately.

Annie used the wrist joints of her wings and her long claws to skitter closer to him, tucking herself under his arm. She pecked tenderly at the week-old silver stubble on his cheek. When he rubbed her chin, her eyelids fluttered in djemon ecstasy. She emitted a sort of chirrupy clucking sound.

Charlie made little kissy noises at her. "I talk to 'er. Read to 'er." He gave me an odd, half-prideful, half apologetic look. "She's smart, I tell ya. Picked it up right quick. I even taught 'er how to sing. You want to hear it?"

Any normal person would know instinctively that the noise a pterodactyl might produce would hardly be called a song, but I couldn't say that to Charlie. It would hurt his feelings. I mean my own djemon, Blix would not win any beauty prizes, but I love him anyway. "Yeah, sure. Let's hear it." I braced myself for the squawk.

Instead, Annie delivered a perfectly charming rendition of 'Twinkle Twinkle Little Star'. Sort of a cross between a parrot and Miss Piggy.

I clapped my hands and she preened with pleasure. "Thank you," she said.

"Oh man, Charlie. How did she—when did she start speaking?"

He unzipped his gear bag and began laying out his clamshells and bundles of sage. "A few weeks ago. Like I told ya, she keeps me comp'ny."

"I know, but...wow." Annie had been even smaller than Blix when I'd given her to him. She balanced on the wrists of her leathery wings and used her long toes like nimble fingers to help him, anticipating his needs. "I wish Blix--."

"Ya got to talk to 'em, Mattie—they need to be part of your life. They learn from watchin' ya. Listenin' to ya. They take it all in. How you get along with other people. Watchin' how you figger stuff out. And ya gotta give 'em a job. "

I couldn't help but notice how attuned Charlie and Annie were to each other. Her sharp eyes followed his every move and anticipated his needs. They were a team.

Nothing like Blix and me. Blix was happiest curled up in my lap. He loved being petted more than anything. Other than pawing at me when he wanted attention, he didn't communicate. He could barely squeak.

Rhys and Henri both had been telling me that I was giving Blix the wrong kind of attention. Rhys said djemons that are coddled and petted become spoiled and self-centered. They needed to feel useful, and he should know, because he used to be one.

Watching Charlie and Annie work together in perfect harmony was a revelation. Maybe I had been spoiling Blix. A little.

Charlie lit the first smudge stick and began to chant. He didn't need me hanging around while he gathered up the restless spirits, any more than I need him when I'm banishing djemons. I pulled the big mag-light out of my canvas bag and headed toward the back of the house to the kitchen.

The basement door was in the kitchen, just as I expected. A length of two by four had been shoved up under the knob as a wedge to keep the door shut.

Like that would stop a poltergeist.

I removed the lumber, and stepped into the stairwell. The lights didn't work down here either, but it wasn't entirely dark. A couple of narrow above-grade basement windows illuminated the gloom with the final dregs of daylight. The crescent on my palm itched like crazy. There was a djemon was down here, all right. I'd have it banished in no time.

It's what I do.

"Are you decent?" I heard a crash and scurrying from below. I had a momentary twinge of fear, but shook it off. Rats, maybe. Or mice. They couldn't hurt me.

Spiders, though. That was another thing entirely.

I flashed the light around, checking for cobwebs. It looked pretty clean down there. I clomped down the stairs into the partially finished basement.

The irregularly-shaped space looked as empty as the rest of the house. I turned slowly, flashing my light around the wide structural columns and into the shadows, reaching out with my senses until the scar on my palm pulsed. I flashed the light into an alcove lined with wine racks—a few dusty bottles left behind by the previous owners. The basement looked as if it hadn't been painted in decades. On the cement floor, shards of a broken wine bottle lay in a puddle as red as blood.

Whatever it was, it was hiding. No matter.

"Here me and obey," I began. Immediately, a pair of yellow eyes peeked down at me from the top of the wine rack.

I flashed the light on him. "Oh, hey. There you are."

It had the bloated face of a toad, a pot-bellied body, and long-fingered hands tipped with hooked claws. It wore a red fez with a black tassel set at a jaunty angle atop its bald head, and a red wool military-style jacket over its grey-brown mottled skin.

It was bigger than Blix. Sheesh, bigger even than Annie. I hadn't run into anything this size in months. I'd never seen him before, but I knew its name.

Zeypax.

This guy belonged to somebody. One of the advantages of being Morta's kin is that I know a djemon's name as soon as I see it. Whoever his owner was, he or she had designated the wine cellar in this empty old house as the place for Zeypax to stay until summoned. Maybe Zeypax belonged to the previous owners, or one of the neighbors. Zeypax had to be the so-called poltergeist that'd been smashing all the light bulbs.

The creature stared down at me with a cold, reptilian glare. "Depart immediately, slovenly trespasser." He sounded like Shakespeare with a mouthful of marbles.

"Hey, don't be rude," I said. "I'm not slovenly, this jacket is a classic. And the jeans are clean."

It bared its teeth. They were small, but pointy-sharp. "Hell is empty and all the devils are here."

"You don't scare me. Who's your master?" I asked.

"Stupid human. Do'st thou think I would tell thee? Begone! Lest my master lay a dire malediction of plagues and pestilence upon thee."

"Yeah, right. Well, I'm the Hand of Fate."

"Signifying nothing," it sneered.

I'd never had djemon address me like this before. With a flex of my fingers, Morta's heavy shears slipped into my hand, giving me a little boost of confidence.

"Flee now the wrath of my exalted master, ere accursed havoc is wreaked upon thee."

"What the frack is the matter with you, anyway?" I snorted. "Are you threatening me?"

It flicked its hand at me dismissively. "Remove thyself from these premises, maggot breath. Thy speech is a malignant canker upon--."

I didn't need to hear the rest. "I hereby banish Zeypax from all physical earthly planes, never to return."

The djemon Zeypax winked out of sight in mid-sentence. *Yeah, baby.*

"Hold that thought, Zeypax," I flipped off the empty space where he'd been perched. *Never to return.* He'd never be able to manifest for his master again. I bet Zeypax's master would tear his hair out wondering why his little pet wouldn't come when he called. Served him right. Good to know there were worse demon masters than me.

I cleaned up the broken wine bottle mess with a wad of paper towels I found in one of the cupboards. It took me a while to get all the glass, but I couldn't leave it—I'm a professional.

I wondered who the djemon belonged to. Must be a real jerk. I made a mental note to find out a little more about the neighbors. Maybe one of them had been using his djemon to scare prospective buyers away.

Of course, if I hadn't banished him so fast maybe I could have forced him to tell me who his master was. I mean, what good was being the Hand of Fate if I didn't use the power, right? I should have said, 'tell me the name of your master'. Not as a question, a command. Yeah, he would have been forced to answer that one. Word choice is everything when it comes to demons. Words matter. Phrasing, too.

I'd just finished spiffing up the place when I heard Charlie calling me from upstairs. The house was dark by this time. He'd already dismissed Annie, and seemed to be in a hurry to leave. Probably needed a smoke.

I locked the door behind us and slipped the key back into the realtor's lockbox.

A sudden gust of night wind howled across the porch, slamming us with dead oak leaves. Tiny lights swirled among the flotsam, bouncing off us like an angry swarm of Styrofoam bees. I squinted against the onslaught, batting them away from me. A strange whooshing sound filled the air—part whisper, part echo, part moan.

Loosah-loosah-oooh...

Charlie grabbed my arm and hauled me off the porch toward the car. The mini-tornado of leaves and lights followed us, even banging against the car windows after we got inside.

"Get us outta here, girlie."

I gunned the engine and Trusty Rusty, my ancient Honda, roared to life. By the time I backed the car out of the long driveway, the dust devil had died down, and the fey lights evaporated. I shifted into gear and the car shot forward.

I stared back at the house. "What the hell was that?"

Charlie rubbed his mouth with a trembling hand. "Hey, watch it!"

"Doh!" I wrenched the wheel to the left, narrowly missing the drainage ditch on the passenger side of the road.

"Sorry," I glanced over at my passenger. "You okay?"

Charlie winced. "I'll live. But back there, that was not good."

My heart pounded with the rush of adrenaline. "Ya think? What just happened?"

"Mebbe I shoulda said somethin' when we walked

in." He rubbed his jaw thoughtfully. "Them spirits was terrified."

I stopped the car. "What are you talking about?"

"This time of year, the veil between the living and the dead thins. Probably shoulda thought about it, before I released 'em. But they was so scared..."

I wondered about the buzzing I'd felt when I put my hand on the railing. "How can spirits be scared? Nothing can hurt the dead. They're lucky that way."

He shook his head. "Somethin' not right about that place. I don't like it. Didn't feel like nothin' I ever I come across before."

I glanced back toward the dark house. Charlie walked with a foot in both the living and the dead. He wasn't the sort to let a few restless spirits spook him. Maybe there was more to it. I put my hand on his shoulder. "Talk to me, Charlie. What just happened?"

"Them spirits I released wasn't lost, Mattie. They was trapped in that staircase. Now I think mebbe lettin' 'em loose might not have been such a good idea. Somethin' about it made me want to leave it alone."

His eyes met mine. "But I couldn't just leave 'em there. Wouldn't be right." He gave a small nod, as if confirming his own statement. "That cold we felt when we went inside was a warning to keep away. Some kind of foreign magic, I think. I think them swamp lights that came after us on the porch was sayin' the same thing."

My stomach churned. "What kind of warning?"

He stared out the window, into the darkness. "Can't say. Somethin's coming. Somethin' bad."

I dropped Charlie off at home and drove over to Mystic Properties to meet my boyfriend, Rhys.

Dr. Rhys Warrick is not only a visiting professor at the University of Rochester, he's an expert on cultural mythology and ancient civilizations. This is mostly due to the fact that he's lived through them. Rhys is a two thousand year-old djenie. Meaning, he was once an immortal djemon, who, having faithfully served his master, became a djenie in human form when his master died.

And oh by the way, a bad ass biker dude and best boyfriend ever.

I pulled up beside his truck just as he was locking up shop. He lives in an apartment above Mystic Properties. I threw my arms around him, savoring his warm, familiar scent. Nothing shakes off a case of the woo-woo willies quite as fast as kissing your hunka-hunka burnin' love.

He kissed me good, running his hands over me until I was practically purring.

And that's the problem.

Rhys is an immortal and I'm not. At some point, we're going to have to break up. The only question is when. I can't stand to think that he would stay with me after I'm old and gray out of some warped sense of duty. It's the big fat elephant in the room between us. Or, one of them, at any rate. It's making me crazy, and I'm too chicken to say anything. He knows I'm not completely comfortable in this relationship.

I think he also suspects that I hadn't told him the whole story of the dreamspiders. It was bad enough I still had nightmares over it; the last thing I wanted to do was talk about it. Something like that could change everything between us. Better to pretend nothing ever happened.

"How did it go?"

"Except for the nasty djemon in the basement, fine." I told him about Charlie getting spooked. "He said there were lost souls trapped in the staircase. Does that make any sense?"

He stiffened. "What do you mean by nasty? Did it come after you?"

I shrugged. "Nasty as in insulting. Pretty colorful vocabulary, too. I wasn't scared."

College professor he may be, but Rhys is also a bad-ass warrior—all too familiar with the evils of men and monsters. He calls me his warrior queen, which is, without a doubt, the highest compliment I've ever received from a man. Don't get me wrong—Rhys is very protective, but at the same time, he convinced me to take lessons from his Qhua Bei Master so that I can be my own bad ass when he's not around. According to Master Foo, I'm nowhere near a bad ass yet. "I banished it. Easy peasy. End of story."

"You've got the heart of a lion, lady." He opened the passenger door of the truck for me and nodded to a brightly-wrapped package, sitting on the passenger seat.

I grinned. "What's this?"

"I bought you a present."

I climbed in and tore at the paper. "You got me a toy?"

He switched on the overhead light in the cab. "No it's a Speak 'n Read tablet. For Blix. Now he can learn to speak. And read. All by himself." He frowned. "You don't like it? He's got to learn to speak, Mattie."

I tried to hide my disappointment. "No, it's not that. I just wasn't expecting it, that's all. The first time a man buys me something and it's for my djemon."

I've been meaning to start teaching Blix, just

as soon as I got chance. Clearly, he didn't think I was serious. That stung. Like it wasn't enough that my whole world had been torn apart over the last few months, and that every time I thought my life was finally getting back to normal, I was faced with something like teaching my frikking djemon how to speak. Too weird. "Henri's the expert. Let him show Blix how to use it."

Rhys shook his head. "Blix is your responsibility. Besides Henri and the guys are leaving Wednesday, right after the party."

Rats. I'd forgotten all about it. Henri was going to spend the winter in Florida, touring with Juno and the band. And I'd agreed to take care of the house. That big old, empty house. Rhys and I had been spending most of our nights together, but he was planning another caving trip to the Finger Lakes before Thanksgiving. I was still having creepy crawly rapist nightmares about dreamspiders. What if another one showed up? Ugga mugga.

"Yeah. Riiight." I ran my hand through my hair. It was growing in fast, but I still wasn't used to it. I'd never had short hair in my life. Every time I looked in the mirror, I didn't recognize myself. Sometimes, I didn't really feel much like me anymore, either.

"What's the matter?"

"Nothing. Not a thing." That man was too smart for his own good. I gave him my best smile. "Can't wait to ah, get started teaching Blix how to speak. I am good. To. Go." I waved at the road and gave him a little let's go signal.

Rhys laid his arms over the top of the steering wheel, and stared straight ahead. "This is what I'm talking about. You're a million miles away right now."

"Sorry." I drummed my fingers on the armrest. "You're right. I guess I have had a lot on my mind."

"Share it with me."

The last time he'd asked, instead of telling him about Lucien Bold, I lied and said I wanted to take dance lessons. And actually, that one had worked out pretty well.

"I was just thinking--." I glanced over at him. I didn't like lying to Rhys. I rubbed my sweaty hands along the tops of my thighs. "Since I'm taking care of the house, while Henri and the band are gone, maybe we could try living together. I mean, really living together. Like you'd move your clothes and stuff over. We'll have the whole place to ourselves."

He'd asked me to move in with him previously, but I'd said no. This was right after he'd come back from Scotland and I was still pretty freaked out by Lucien Bold and the whole dreamspider experience. I felt ugly inside and out. I'd been terrified to be alone, but at the same time, I didn't want Rhys, to touch me. I told him I didn't feel comfortable at his place. It was right on a busy street, and there was a lot of traffic and noise from the bars that went on late at night. Rhys didn't like spending the night at Henri's house because of the lack of privacy, and he was right about that. Sharing a house with a vampire rock band is more like living in a frat house than a love nest.

"That is a great idea." Rhys shifted the truck into gear and winked at me. "Let's do it."

"Can't wait," I said, and for the life of me, I didn't know if I was telling the truth or not.

CHAPTER 2

EIGHTH-GRADERS ARE a tough crowd.

From my position behind the center stage podium, I stared across a sea of glassy-eyed eighth graders at Pope Street Middle School's Gymnasium, and just kept yammering away. If I had the trike with me, the kids would have been all over it, but Principal Williams wouldn't let me bring it into the gym. Not a friendly face in the place. Principal Williams' sour expression told me he didn't think much of my speech, either. Dang that Lacey Lippman; nobody told me to bring swag for the kids.

Sheesh, a roomful of zombies would be better than this.

High School graduation rates in Shore Haven being what they were; the Monroe County Schools

Superintendent had initiated the Career Daze program for eighth graders to "light the spark of inspiration in the tender minds of students before they enter high school." Every Friday, local professionals came to speak to the kids about their jobs. This week, it was my turn.

"One of the best things about being a parking control officer is that you get to ride the trike."

"You mean scooter," said a kid in the back. A couple kids snickered.

I gritted my teeth and kept smiling. "No, it's a three-wheeled motorcycle."

"Like a Big Wheel."

Every kid in the room thought that was hilarious. Even the Principal got a kick out of that one.

I finished the rest of my speech in record time. I don't think I inspired a lot of future civil servants. I released my death grip on the podium, smoothing my sweaty hands across my thighs. "Any questions?"

The room went quiet. I tried to catch the eye of one of the kids I knew, Nate Briscoe, but he refused to look at me. I didn't blame him. I was about to make my escape when there was a flicker of movement in the crowd—a hand shot up.

"Yes, Ryan," Principal Williams nodded. "Did you have a question for Officer Blackman?"

A freckle-faced kid with nerdy glasses stood up and pointed at me. "What's wrong with your hand?"

I blushed furiously as a hundred and forty-two kids suddenly pricked up their ears and put me squarely in their sights. Great.

I held up both my hands like it wasn't a big deal. My entire left hand and most of my forearm up to the elbow looked like I'd dipped it into a bucket of black ink. When I wore my jacket and motorcycle gloves, the stain unnoticeable, but I'd left them on my chair.

"I got bit by a spider. The poison left a mark on my skin. The doctor says it'll fade eventually." I knew different, though. The poison trapped beneath my skin was part of me now, like the crescent moon scar or Morta's shears.

"Did it hurt?" asked a girl in the third row.

"Yeah, it did."

"My brother got bit by a spider and it didn't turn his foot black."

"This was a pretty big frikkin' spider."

The class started to throw out more questions, but the principal put an end to it, saying "Thank you, Officer Blackman."

I stepped off the stage to scattered applause and took my seat in the front row below the stage. The entire student body was between me and the exit—there was no way to sneak out before the program was over.

Next up was Honey Briscoe, the owner of Honey Bee's Bakery. She'd brought two dozen boxes of fresh donuts to pass around. Honey had the kids literally eating out of the palm of her hand. A willowy, stunner of woman, she was about ten years older than me. I always thought she could have been a dancer, or even a model, but she married Nate Briscoe as soon as they graduated high school. Warm brown skin, doe eyes, and broad cheekbones gave hints of her mixed African and Senequois heritage.

She started the bakery seven years ago, after her husband, Nate Senior, was killed in the line of duty. The shop had been a hit from day one—in part, because every cop and sheriff's deputy working east of Rochester bought their donuts at Honey Bee's.

She had two boys: eighth-grade Nate Junior, who had pretended he didn't know me, and nine-year old Ray, who everyone called Arby. My brother Lance and his wife used to live just up the street from the Briscoes. My niece Mina and Arby played together when they were toddlers, until Lance's marriage broke up and Violet moved out, taking Mina with her.

Honey explained how she used a lot of math in her recipes and to calculate how much to charge for a donut. She even showed the kids how to twist dough to make pretzels. And when she smiled, the whole room smiled right back at her. By the time she was done, the kids gave her a standing ovation.

Personally, I think they were just on a sugar high from all the donuts. I made a mental note to bring food if I were ever called to do a career day presentation again. Pretty hard to top chocolate donuts, but I bet a pizza would do the trick. Not much chance of topping that.

I was wrong.

Tony Perez, one of the pro soccer players from the Rochester Rhinos, juggled a soccer ball with his feet the whole time he spoke. He was laid-back and charming, with a grin that lit up the room. At the end of his speech he handed out little hacky sack soccer balls with the team logo on it for all the kids. Sheesh, they liked him even better than Honey.

The kids were all kicking around their new soccer sacks, and couldn't wait to leave. I thanked my lucky stars that the final presenter never showed up. I'd fallen off the sugar wagon big-time. The three donuts I'd eaten were making me sleepy and restless at the same time.

Without warning, the gym door slammed opened, and Lydia Fewkes rushed in. She dumped one of two large cloth bags she was carrying onto the empty seat next to me, and then stepped up onto the stage. She apologized to everyone for being late, but the natives were already restless.

Eighth graders are a really tough crowd.

I didn't know her, but I knew who she was. She and her brother, John owned a fancy flower shop, located across the street from Dave's Killer Burgers. It was one of those snooty places, with trendy European antiques, dried herbs, and a tea shop in the back. The flowers were an afterthought, I think. Very popular with tourists. I'd never been inside their shop—I don't buy antiques, flowers, herbs, or tea. Not my kind of place. But their seasonal display windows were lavishly decorated, and this month's fall theme was lit with tiny white lights, brightly-colored leaves, pumpkins, and fairy gardens.

"I'm Liddy," she said, by way of introduction. "My brother and I own of Lotus Floral & Apothecary, but I think several of you might recognize me as the puppet lady. My Saturday morning puppet shows in the display window of our shop have gotten quite popular."

A scatter of enthusiastic clapping confirmed her story.

"When Mr. Williams asked me to come here today, I think he imagined I would speak to you as a small business owner, but instead, I am going to speak to you about the life of an artist."

She certainly looked the part. Jeweled flower barrettes sparkled like blood rubies in her long, wavy brown hair. She wore a knee length, turquoise, red, and grey gypsy skirt that looked as if it had been stitched together from antique scarves. Suede cowboy boots with silver conches along the side, and an open knit sweater worn over a lacy camisole completed her funky-cool look.

Must be nice to wear whatever she wanted to work. I glanced down at my navy uniform and square-toed boots, and took solace in my job security. Well, except for this year, when the budget had forced cutbacks. I couldn't afford cool clothes like that, even if I wanted to--*which I didn't*. Although those boots were pretty bad ass.

Sweet, rather than pretty, Liddy made the most of what she had with make-up, using it to accentuate her expressive eyes. She said she'd been a stage actress in England, and I could certainly believe it. Anyone could see she had star quality.

She talked about theatre, costuming, acting, and her lifelong fascination with hand-carved wooden dolls and puppetry. She was animated and lively. I couldn't help but envy her.

From her oversized cloth bag, Liddy brought out one of the marionettes she'd made. It was an elephant—complete with saggy knees and waggly ears. While she spoke about her life as an artist, the elephant seemed to come alive under her hands. It interrupted her with questions—its long trunk pulling on her skirt or reaching for her long hair. Pretty cute.

Okay, maybe even adorable.

Then, as if noticing the audience for the first time, the elephant winked at the kids and started doing a little hip-hop dance step until Liddy stopped talking. She asked the kids if they wanted to see more, and by this time those fickle little eighth graders were putty in her hands. Liddy and the little elephant did a rap song and jive routine about finding your passion and staying in school—just the right level for the kids. The rap beat was irresistible and the words were really clever. Every kid in the gym was on their feet, entranced by the dancing marionette—even the principal was nodding along to the beat.

I admit it--I couldn't stop my feet from stepping to the music, either. Rhys and I had started taking a dance class—Dancing for Lovers—and I had a whole new appreciation for all kinds of music.

I must've jostled the chair next to me, because Liddy's other bag, which she'd dumped next to me, fell to the floor, spewing scraps of brightly colored cloth, spools of thread, and dozens of clear packets of dried herbs out onto the linoleum. I leaned down to pick up the mess.

I gathered up the spilled fabric to shove it back in the bag. There was another wooden puppet inside. The lovely painted face of a dark-haired boy stared up at me. Its charming painted features were cracked and nearly worn off with age. He was dressed in some sort of a carnival costume. So beautiful. Probably worth a lot of money. Its hair had gotten mussed in the fall.

I smoothed the dark locks away from the doll's face, marveling at the seemingly real hair. The crescent scar on the palm of my hand began to itch.

Help me, Morta! Help me!

I dropped the doll and bag both like a hot potato, strewing pins, thread spools, and glass beads across the floor. I looked round, but the kids were too busy rappin' to the beat of the elephant stomping it up on stage. The voice was only in my mind.

I shoved the spillage back into the bag. My hand hovered over the wood puppet for a moment, and then picked it up again.

I call upon the Hand of Fate to—.

The door in my mind linking me to Morta was thrown open. The crescent scar on the palm of my hand burned like fire. I dropped the doll and kicked it into the open sack.

Was it alive? No, of course not. It was just a doll. Too many chocolate donuts, that's all.

I glanced up and saw Liddy Fewkes staring daggers at me from the stage. The audience was still clapping to the beat, even as Liddy ended the performance and shoved the elephant marionette into her bag. The kids shouted and cheered as she stepped away from the podium, but she kept her eyes on me.

"Let's give Miss Fewkes and all our guests a big round of applause," said Principal Williams.

Liddy gave a final wave and stepped off the stage, a wooden smile glued on her face.

I'd managed to shove most of the rest of the junk back into the sack before Liddy got to me.

"I'll take *that*." She snatched the bag from me and muscled her way through the crowd.

Jeeze Laweeze, lady. No need to be so huffy about it. I don't think I could have stopped her, even if I tried. Every kid in the gym was on their feet now, eager to scarf up the last of the free donuts.

Long after Liddy Fewkes left the building, the voice in my head kept screaming.

CHAPTER 3

SATURDAY MORNING, I begged off practice with Master Foo to spend time with Blix and the new Speak and Read tablet Rhys had given me. Rhys and Henri were both crazy about their Qhua Bei workouts. However, my lessons with Master Foo, the martial arts instructor usually, usually left me feeling inadequate.

I sat at the kitchen table; the colorful plastic tablet and my cell phone positioned in front of me. Blix perched on my left wrist, his ears perked, his expression intense. He kept looking from me to the tablet and back again.

I showed him how to turn it on, and when the screen came up, there was a picture of an apple. It had a big pink capital "A" next to it, and the word, "apple" spelled out underneath. I tapped the picture, and a simulated voice said, "A is for Apple. Say apple."

Blix looked up at me and gave a muted squeak.

"This will teach you how to talk, Blix." I pointed to my phone. "It's just like my cell phone, but this one is for you."

I showed him how to use the different buttons for different lessons—for both the alphabet and counting. The program gave him two chances to say the word correctly before moving onto the next letter.

He tapped the tablet tentatively with a long claw. Blix's back feet were padded claws like a cat's. His front feet were shaped a bit like monkey hands, tipped with long sharp talons—a combination both dexterous and deadly.

In less than five minutes, he was already up to P is for Pony. Smart little djemon. He didn't any help to figure it out. I told him he was a good boy and he actually chirruped a little, but his eyes never left the tablet. When I left, Blix was still tap-tap-tapping away on the key pad. I admit, seeing him take to it so fast made me feel pretty good. He'd be speaking in no time. Rhys and Henri would be so impressed.

Time for breakfast.

Killer Dave's had been closed for months, so I walked down to Honey Bee's for coffee and a chocolate croissant. Nate Junior was working the counter by himself this morning. I stepped up and placed my order.

"Sorry, Miss Blackman, we're all out of chocolate croissants this morning."

Just my luck. I perused the display shelves. Now that I'd fallen off the sugar wagon, I needed chocolate with my coffee. Cinnamon rolls and maple bars just weren't going to cut it.

Honey swooshed out from the back with a fresh tray of her special muffins topped with a dollop of cream-cheese icing. They're more like a cupcake for grownups. Still warm from the oven, they smelled like banana-walnut heaven.

"Morning, Mattie," Honey said. "You're too late for the croissants. How about a dozen chocolate donuts? I know Henri likes those too."

After the Career Daze incident, I'd decided to go cold turkey on the chocolate donuts. "A muffin will be fine."

"That's it?" She gave me a little pout. "Are you sure?"

"Yeah, I'm trying to cut back. And a coffee. For here." I pointed to the empty table nearest the kitchen.

I paid Nate and took my coffee and muffin over to the table. Honey took the other seat with a muffin for herself.

"You don't mind if I join you, do you? These are my absolute favorites. I only make them once a week. Otherwise I'd be big as a house."

"I don't believe it for a minute," I grinned and poked my finger in the swirl of icing on the top of my muffin. *Nummy*. "You could be a model."

"Well, aren't you sweet?" She bit into the crunchy muffin top, getting a smear of icing on her upper lip, which she wiped away discreetly with her napkin.

I followed suit and immediately understood why the muffins were her favorites. The cake was tender and moist and at the same time crunchy with walnut chunks. Ooh, and that icing—maybe chocolate was a little overrated.

"You were a hit with the kids on Career Day," I said.

She laughed. "Any kid with a donut in his hand is a happy kid. I could have stood up there and recited the Gettysburg Address and they would've been happy to hear it."

"At least they listened. Next time I'll bring swag."

"Liddy Fewkes didn't brink swag."

Something in Honey's expression caught me. I took a sip of coffee. "No. The kids sure liked her, though," I said.

A moment stretched between us. Honey pushed

42

her muffin away, half-eaten. "Well."

I got the feeling that she had a lot more to say. "How well do you know her?"

She took a deep breath and shrugged, not looking at me. "I'm too busy to get out much. She's really got a knack for those puppets, though. I never liked puppets when I was a kid. I always thought they were creepy." She shivered. "But Arby is mad for them. I can't keep him away from those Saturday shows of hers."

I stared at her. It felt as if she was saying something I was supposed to understand. I thought about the puppet in the bag. Had she seen something? Had she heard the puppet speak to me? Impossible.

I knew Honey, but not well enough to figure out what she was saying. "Do you know something?"

She shook her head, as if I'd missed the point and she didn't want to explain it. "Nothing relevant. Say, Lou tells me you're working together."

Safer territory. "Yeah, he's teaching me investigative techniques. Gave me a book and everything."

"Well, I'm glad to hear it. Being a meter maid has got to be a sucky job. You can do better."

"Hey, don't say that! It's a perfectly respectable way to make a living."

She gave me an amused look. "I see. So, they're

paying you now?"

"Well, okay, yeah. The city budget has been a little dicey lately. But I'll be working full-time again come spring. I hope."

She shook her head. "Look girl, anybody else would have taken the hint and quit months ago. Lou is a good man—a cunning man, and the best partner my husband ever had. You can learn a lot from him." She put her hand on my arm. "You two make a good match."

"It's not like that," I said. "Lou and I are friends and colleagues, but that's all. I've already got a boyfriend."

"Ah. You and Rhys then." She nodded knowingly.

I blushed. I didn't know if she knew Rhys was and immortal djenie or not. "I mean, Lou's great, but I'm not looking for a husband."

"He's been a wonderful to me and the kids. You can trust him, Mattie."

"That's high praise, coming from you." Honey was good people. I liked her even better for telling me what she thought of Lou.

A bit of tension I didn't realize I'd been holding onto suddenly eased. Lou was a great guy, but it was good to hear it from someone who had every reason to hate him. I'd all but forgotten that Nate Briscoe had died taking a bullet meant for Lou.

CHAPTER 4

"EVERYBODY LIES, MATTIE. It doesn't mean they're cheating."

It was a midnight. Lou and I were on a stakeout, sitting in his beat-up Subaru station wagon, watching the driveway of a split-level ranch from our parking spot in front of a house three doors away. The client was out of town visiting her parents with the kiddies, and we were there to make sure there was no hubby hanky-panky going on. Lou preferred to do stakeouts in my black Honda, because at night, his white Subaru was too visible, but my not so Trusty Rusty was in the shop again.

We'd been sitting here for hours. It looked like hubby was pretty much down for the count. Lou was paying me, so I couldn't really complain. He'd been quizzing me on the book he'd given me, called *Private Investigation Made Easy*. I hadn't actually read it yet.

"Come on, this is an easy one. Give me three signs of partner infidelity." His gaze never left the house we were watching.

I licked Cheeto dust off my fingers. I was back on the no sugar wagon, having traded my chocolate donut addiction for the fine line of snack products marketed by Frito-Lay.

"Okay. Phone hang-ups. "

"What else?"

I held up the bag. "Cheeto?"

Lou and I go way back. Back to when I first got hired by the City. Parking control was always sort of looked down upon by Picston PD, but Nate and Lou always waved hello whenever they passed me on duty. Lou took it pretty hard when Nate was killed. He stayed on the job for a few more years, but you could tell his heart wasn't in it. When they offered him early retirement, he took it and opened his own private investigation business.

"Come on."

Mostly, he takes clients from Shore Haven's supernatural community. They trust him because he's one of them. I don't know exactly what he is, but he doesn't have a lifeline. He's not the kind of guy who stands out in a crowd, either. He spent his whole career working with cops and none of them ever realized how good Lou is with secrets. Running his own PI business is perfect for him. And lucky for me, too.

"Um, unusual credit card charges."

"Go on," he said.

"Like flower shop charges when she doesn't get the flowers. Or sexy lingerie. Or if he starts hiding the bills."

"Or she," Lou prompted. "Although in my experience, women tend to be more careful about their credit card purchases."

I popped another Cheeto in my mouth. "Why all the cheating spouse cases?"

He shrugged. "It pays the bills. Far less chance of finding dead bodies than in missing persons cases."

I shuddered, remembering Wiley Willy's desiccated corpse.

The house lights in the split ranch we were watching went out. "Here we go." Lou said. "If the wife's hunch is correct, whatever is going to happen should happen soon."

"How often is the wife right?"

"Once one partner starts keeping secrets, the other one senses it pretty quick and wants to know why."

I nodded, not taking my eyes off the house. Thank

goodness Rhys and I had no more secrets from each other. Except that one thing about Luçien Bold. A guilty blush warmed my cheeks.

Down the street, the garage door opened, and the cheating hubby rolled down the driveway in the family Volvo station wagon with the headlights turned off.

"Well, well." I crumpled up the empty bag of Cheetos. I pulled a dollar bill out of the pocket of my jeans and passed it over to Lou. "You called it."

"Right on schedule," Lou said. "Let that be a lesson for you. Never doubt a woman who suspects her husband is up to something."

"Cynic," I said.

He waited until the car reached the stop sign at the end of the street and hubby turned on the headlights, before turning the key on the ignition. Lou always insisted on driving whenever we worked together. He said my driving made him nervous.

"Now pay attention, Mattie. Tailing a car at this time of night can be tricky. The most important aspect of moving vehicle surveillance is keeping enough cover between you and the car you're tailing."

"Well, duh. Hurry up, you're gonna lose him—you drive like an old lady."

"Better we lose him than he spots us. A guy who spots a tail is unpredictable, and far more prone to violence. If not to us, than to others."

I had my foot to the floor of the passenger side of the car, but Lou kept our speed to an agonizingly slow twenty-five miles an hour.

We followed the Volvo through Penfield, nearly all the way to Webster. Lou stayed so far behind, I could have sworn we'd lost him more than once. We were out on Plank Road, amid the apple orchards south of Knutt's Apple Farm. Way out in the boonies where there were no streetlights. Up ahead, the Volvo made a sudden right and drove up an empty dirt track.

Lou turned off the headlights and edged the Subaru over to the shoulder, nosing his way under the heavy branches of a spreading blue spruce. "This is it." He reached into the back seat and grabbed our jackets. "We're going to have to hoof it from here."

"This is a tractor road. What's he doing out here?" I kept my voice low.

Lou didn't answer.

This part of Webster is aggressively rural--hardly the place for a romantic tryst. Neither a porch light nor curtained window cut the darkness. With nothing but the sliver of a moon and stars to light our way, we stumbled up the deeply grooved dirt track. Lou had to be as curious as I was.

The Volvo was parked at the end of a long line

of cars. The trail curved to the left, and led to the hulking silhouette of an old abandoned barn. As one, we stopped, our ears strained for the answer to the mystery. Where were they?

Waist-high dried weeds surrounded the structure. Dimly, I could see a path cut through the vegetation on one side of the barn, leading around to the back. I pointed to it and Lou led the way.

Something in the setup warned us both to be quiet; not an easy thing to do when walking through dry thistles. Lou moved surely, silent as a stalking cat. I tried to step where he stepped. My heart pounded as we rounded the barn, but there was nothing to see.

He froze, his head cocked to listen. From up ahead, a low murmur of voices sounded through the trees. The exact direction of the voices was difficult to determine. We moved toward the orchard, leaving the crunch and grasp of thistles behind us.

It was easier going here. Most of the apple trees had lost their leaves to the first frost of the season. The litter beneath our feet had softened to mulch from recent rains. I pulled the collar of my jacket up to ward off the night chill. We climbed steadily, until we crested the hill behind the orchard. Below us, the land gave way to an old cemetery, hidden in a shallow vale.

Lou and I stood like statues, our bodies straining for the slightest sound. He held his hand out for silence. Even in the dark, I could tell the cemetery had been long neglected. Headstones lay tumbled askew and broken, partially hidden in the overgrown grass. The sound of voices was clearer here. It was coming from behind a memorial vault as big as a truck.

Using the structure as cover, we eased our way down the wet, grassy slope to the vault for a better look.

At the bottom of the vale, a dozen or so dark-robed, hooded figures, stood in a circle around a gnarled old tree, holding hands as they chanted in a language I didn't understand. Latin, maybe. We were too far away to hear the words, but light from several small lanterns illuminated the scene with a soft glow. In the center of the circle, next to the tree, a lone figure seemed to be doing some sort of conducting— waving a long twig in one hand, and a small knife in the other.

Pagans. I rolled my eyes. What a letdown. Unless they were naked under those robes, which I seriously doubted, given how frikking cold it was out here, the hubby we'd followed wasn't a cheater, he was a witch. Monroe County had more than its share of them. Wiccans. Druids. Tree huggers. Wifey wife had nothing to worry about.

Lou tapped me on the shoulder and jerked his head back toward the way we'd come, his expression troubled. He had me doing double time to keep up on the way back. Once we reached the barn, I hissed at him to slow down.

"Don't tell me you're scared of a few pagans."

"No, not pagans. They're a cult." We'd reached the dirt track, and it was easier going. "At one time, the Penfield witches was the oldest organized coven in North America. There are no witches in that coven anymore."

"Where did they go?"

"In the last decade, the group has been taken over by a couple of sorcerers, dedicated to practicing the black arts. As a group, they're aggressive, arrogant, and coercive. The cult has managed to place their people in influential positions in local government. The Sheriff has his hands tied—forced to turn a blind eye to their shenanigans." He wiped his sweaty forehead on his sleeve. "I've been searching for their meeting place for years, and never found it. We weren't supposed to see that."

"What were they doing?"

"It's called layering." He shook his head and picked up the pace again. "Building up a reservoir of power. It's like filling up a gas tank. I haven't seen anything like that in a very long time."

I'd lived in Monroe County all my life and never heard of the Penfield witches. "I don't get it. If they want to hang out in an abandoned cemetery all night, what's the big deal?"

"These aren't the pagan witches you think they are—although they used to be. They're occultists—dedicated to the study of ancient rituals for the purposes of gaining power."

"You're not making sense, Lou."

"This layering is serious business. They're doing it for a reason. The only reason I can think of is to summon a demon. Maybe even a deity. Very dark stuff."

"Come on, Lou. You don't need a summoning circle to get a demon—even I know that."

"I'm not talking about *djinn*, Mattie. I'm talking about deities. Devils. Drudes. Goblins. Incubi and Succubi. Creatures of the Abyss." He stopped so suddenly I ran right into him. He grabbed me by my shoulders and glared at me—so close, I could feel the heat of his anger. "They're messing with things they cannot possibly control. I know black magic when I see it. It's like you and djemons, Mattie. That's *my* legacy. You're just going to have to trust me on this."

"Okay, okay. I got it." Sheesh.

"Let's get out of here before they see us." He moved quickly—I had to run to keep up.

We'd reached the line of cars. Lou pulled out his cell phone and snapped photos of the license plates on the vehicles we'd passed on the way in.

"What are you going to tell the wife? Do you think she's a witch too?"

He stiffened. "Damn. If the wife is one of them, maybe this was a set-up. I can't tell her anything. I'll give her a refund; tell her I didn't find anything."

"Don't go paranoid, on me, Lou. We just spent seven hours on stakeout, and you want to throw it away? What the hell?"

"You're damn right I do," he said. "I don't want to give them anything that will lead them back to us. I've been looking for this place for years, Mattie. That's why I'm taking pics of these plate numbers."

I'd never seen this side of Lou before. "I don't get it. So they're sorcerers, what's the big deal? Why are you so upset?"

"These people are bad news. I mean it. Stay away from them, Mattie. Promise me. You don't want anything to do with them. They're a cult. Smart and organized and messing with things they shouldn't be. Once they get their claws in you they'll never let you go. Best to just stay clear. Promise me you'll have nothing to do with them."

We'd reached the car. "Yeah, okay. Fine."

"Say it. Say you'll drop this. I want your word." The sour scent of cold fear clung to him.

Lou wasn't the type to get spooked. I held up my hands in supplication. "Okay, I promise." I made a mental note to ask Rhys about black sorcerers.

A pair of headlights coming up Plank Road hit us.

Lou grabbed me, pulling me into the deeper shadows beneath the spruce tree. He pushed me up against the car, wrapping his arms around me, his lips pressed against my neck.

"Whatever happens, don't let them see your face," he said. I felt Lou's fear and obeyed.

An old pickup truck slowed to a crawl, then stopped at the turnoff, less than a dozen feet away. I threw my arms around Lou's neck and followed his example, running my hands up and down his back, like a lover in the throes of passion.

The truck idled there for a full minute, the number four piston ticking in perfect time with the pounding of my heart. I squeezed my eyes shit against the glare of the headlights and wrapped my leg around Lou's hip, pulling him closer. A few more long seconds ticked by, then the truck turned left and moved slowly up the dirt drive we'd just walked down.

Lou released me, his eyes focused on the truck's retreating taillights. "That was too close. Let's get out of here."

CHAPTER 5

ON WEDNESDAY, I stopped by Aapex Bike and Auto to pick up my car.

"Sorry, Mattie, ignition system was shorted out," Doc said. He and my brother Lance used to own the business together. Doc was like one of the family. "Never seen that in a Honda before. It's going to need to be replaced. The parts are special order."

"Oh come on. I can't keep taking the bus." I hated not having my own wheels. Doc would never understand how humiliating it was for me to take bus in my city parking control uniform, carrying my helmet under my arm. The sly comments and jibes weren't funny anymore. "Can't you give me a loaner?"

"Hah! You forget I'm the one who has to keep putting that piece of shit you call a Honda back together all the time. No way."

"Oh, man, that's not fair." It stung like hell to admit it, but in the last year, Doc had seen more of my car than I had. "You said it yourself. It wasn't fault. Not this time."

He wiped his hands on a faded shop rag. "Tell you what. I can let you borrow the Vic for a few days."

My heart skipped a beat. "You're giving me my bike back?"

Trusty Rusty was my transport, but the Victory Hammer S motorcycle was my pride and joy. I'd traded it to Doc for the repairs on Rusty last time around. It had been a gift from Lance. The bike is built a little wider and lower to the ground than most road bikes—making it perfect for women like me. Doc is too tall for it, and his wife prefers her Harley, so it was just sitting in his glass-walled showroom, as shiny and clean as the day I brought it in.

A totally kick-ass bike. I wished I'd never let it go. "Oh man, that's great. Thanks, Doc. You're the best!"

He handed me the key, a near-smile curling at the corner of his mouth. "If it snows, bring her right back."

I kissed the key. "Of course." No one in their right mind would let a bike like that out on the road where the salt could hurt it. October already, and we hadn't seen our first snow yet. The whole region had been experiencing a long run of good weather. Maybe Rhys and I could take a road trip out to Letchworth State park on the weekend to see the fall colors.

I strapped my helmet on and walked the bike out of the showroom, grinning like a jack-o-lantern. I threw my leg over the bike and a moment later, the thrum of the Vic's engine purred between my legs. For the first time in months, I felt strong and sexy and ready to conquer the world.

That night, Rhys and I arrived at Maestro's Dance studio a little before 8pm. The studio, located in the warehouse section of Germantown, was two blocks down from the meat-packing plant. Eight-foot-tall picture windows faced the street. The interior walls were all mirrored. The ceilings and open ductwork had all been painted dark maroon. Polished wood floors and amber soffit lighting made the large space seem warm and intimate, rather than intimidating.

This was our fifth of eight lessons in the Dancing for Lovers class. Rhys and I showed up in our usual tee-shirts, boots, and jeans. The other five couples there were dressed more formally; the men in sports jackets and the women in skirts. Aside from the part about Rhys being a couple of thousand years old, we were younger than the five other dance partners, most of whom were in their mid-forties and fifties.

Tonight, Mr. Maestro's assistant, Stella, greeted us wearing a skin-tight black leotard, fishnet tights, and spike heels. Trim and curvy, without an ounce of jiggle, she was always cheerful and welcoming. Every inch of her perfectly coiffed blonde hair had been shellacked in place with hairspray.

"Welcome, welcome. I hope you've all been practicing." She checked our names off on the attendance sheet.

As if by some secret signal, Mr. Maestro entered the studio. He clapped his hands for our attention. He had an interesting, if ageless face. His sharp eyes scanned the room, restless and predatory as a wolf looking to spot the weakest in the herd. He wore his usual, skin-tight black stretch pants, with a white shirt open to his waist over a black turtleneck, and white spats on his shoes. Smarmy guy. If you looked up the word, lothario in the dictionary, that was Mr. Maestro.

But after our first lesson, Rhys and I both knew he was a hell of a good teacher. He and Stella were both vamps, but Rhys told me that Mr. Maestro was a different kind of vampire, in that he fed off people's emotions. The more powerful, the better.

"Listen up children," Mr. Maestro announced, his restless fingers fluttering in the air. "Tonight we will put the steps we've been working on to music. Please watch and learn as Stella and I demonstrate the music of love, Tango Jive."

With that, he struck a pose and lifted his hand to Stella. She hit the 'play' button on the remote, and moved gracefully across the floor to take his hand.

A heavy base drumbeat filled the room—the studio had a great sound system. The pair went into action, a palpable vibe of sensuality between them. The couple moved as one, starting out slow, wrapped in each other's arms, twisting and turning in perfect harmony, then, as the music changed tempo, they matched it perfectly. Stella and Maestro stared deeply into each other's eyes, never once looking at their feet or where they were going—they were totally focused on each other. Watching them together, moving to the hot beat of that music had me wanting to be part of it, too. The beat transitioned again, and there was daylight between them, but it was only so that they could move like a pair of dervishes—back and forth, crossing and twirling, separately, yet both of them in perfect synchronicity.

I couldn't take my eyes off them.

Dancing—at least the kind of dancing that Mr.

Maestro and Stella taught—required utter trust between the partners, because at any one time, one or the other partner would be in total control of the couple's forward movement. The music grew to a climax, and everyone in the room could see they were enjoying every second of it, and that for them, the world had faded away—save for the music, the beat, and each other.

Rhys and I had both gone into the whole dance lessons thing as a bit of a lark, but watching these two was no joke. Every time they demonstrated the steps for us, they looked so effortless. Watching them dance made me feel a bit like a voyeur—like what they were showing us was too private, too personal, and too risqué to stare at openly.

I was envious of them. I wanted that. And after the first lesson, Rhys confessed to me that he envied them too. We'd made a pact to take it seriously, and discovered that Dancing for Lovers with Mr. Maestro and Stella was a blast.

When it ended, the class broke out into wild applause. The pair bowed and I caught another glimpse of fang from Stella.

"And now it is your turn," Maestro addressed the class. "When we started, I guaranteed that each and every one of you would be able to perform the steps we've demonstrated here tonight." He blotted a bit of moisture from his brow with a handkerchief. "And that and your partner would reach a higher level of intimacy every week. Tonight, you are going to show us how far you've come."

For the next forty-five minutes, he and Stella ran us through a warm-up of three different combinations of steps, strung out in a line across the dance floor. Each of the three series of steps required our utmost attention to the count, foot placement, and body position. The first week had been rough, but Rhys and I moved through the warm-up easily now, moving both backwards and forwards to the beat. It was a great workout.

Mr. Maestro then cleared the floor of all but one couple and started the music. Each couple danced to a different song, one we hadn't heard before. At the end of each couple's routine, he offered suggestions for improvement.

I felt more than a little nervous when it was our turn. Rhys led me to the center of dance floor. He slipped his hand around my back and pulled me close. He was warm and so was I, and as we waited for the music to begin, we both grinned with anticipated pleasure. Rhys was every bit as happy to have me pressed up against him as I was to be there.

The sound of drums in the intro built up into an irresistible, throbbing beat. We weren't perfect, but as we rock-stepped, triple-stepped, triple-step, rock-stepped around the room, and the muscle memory that Mr. Maestro had been telling us about for the past several weeks kicked in—I didn't even need to think about what I was doing. I followed Rhys's every move, and his steps mirrored mine. I loved the sensation of sliding my hands across his rock-hard stomach and cupping his great ass. His hands were bold—stroking my thighs, my hips, and the small of my back. He threw me away and caught me—by my fingers, my waist, and neck. The beat of the drums thrummed in our bones until that was all there was. The rest of the class faded away, and it was just me and Rhys and the beat and the heat and a spark between us that hadn't been there before.

When the music stopped, it caught us both by surprise. Even Mr. Maestro joined into the applause, saying, "And that, ladies and gentlemen, is how it's done."

CHAPTER 6

THURSDAY NIGHT WAS Henri's bon voyage party at Growlers Pizza, a werewolf joint out on Five Mile Road in Penfield. Even by werewolf standards, the bar was a dive, but they did allow vampires, and the pizza was supposed to be good.

The pub was a long, low brick building with a bright green door—utterly lacking any sort of character. The parking lot was already full, so Rhys parked the truck right along Five Mile, right behind Lou's white Subaru. We dodged heavy highway traffic crossing Five Mile, arriving at the restaurant a little breathless.

The scent of pizza and beer greeted us at the door, along with the usual din of the jukebox, pinball machines, and the too-loud banter of customers. Henri, Juno Rockover, Ray Mackie, Mike Weyland and the rest of the Rogues and their roadies were already seated at a long table set up against the back wall. Lou was there, and I recognized Herman the German, and Dr. Jensen, the crypto-vet.

"Mattie, Rhys, over here!" Henri waved us over. He was positively exuberant. Even the vamps seemed in good spirits. The vamps didn't eat or drink, but that didn't seem to stop them from enjoying themselves. You haven't lived until you've seen a roomful of vamps wearing silly paper crowns.

Winters in upstate New York are brutal, and a lot of local vamps spend their winters in Florida. Juno had rented a big house for the band in Clearwater. It was going to be like one big winter-long party, and Henri was looking forward to his first big adventure. Rhys had warned me that all new djenies go through long phases of wanderlust, and that I shouldn't try to change his mind about leaving. After seeing how happy he was in his relationship with Juno, I didn't have the heart to do anything but wish him good luck.

The waitress brought over another large pepperoni, still hot from the oven, and set it down right in front of me. Before Lou could grab it, I snagged the first slice--the gooey cheese strings dragged all the way to my plate. Thin crust, my favorite.

A sudden hush fell over the bar. The jukebox went

silent. Two women stood in the entrance, looking stiff and out of place. Both were dressed in jeans, Buffalo Bills team jackets, and heavy steel-toed boots. The taller of the two wore her long brown hair bound up in a topknot, while the shorter sported a spiky blue Mohawk and a dozen or more silver rings pierced the edge of each ear.

They stared at our table with open hostility. Belinda the waitress looked terrified. Everyone at the table seemed just as mystified as me.

A low rumble sounded from the guys shooting pool. One of the pool players began to boo, and the other patrons picked it up, until the sound rose to a howl.

Kevin, the bartender yelled, "Enough!" The howling stopped immediately and rowdies quieted. He grabbed a baseball bat from behind the bar and stalked toward the women.

"We don't serve your kind here," he said. He wasn't shouting, but in the dead quiet of the bar, his voice carried.

"Good, 'cause we sure as hell didn't come for the food." Blue Mohawk sneered. "We're looking for somebody."

The crescent-shaped scar on the palm of my hand began to tingle.

"Get out." Kevin shifted his grip on the bat.

"Better watch your mouth, Kev," the tall one said. "If you know what's good for you."

"You threaten me in my own place?" Kevin's voice dropped to a low rumble. He set the bat carefully on the bar.

The air went out of the room. A wave of adrenaline and testosterone from the dozen or so werewolves at the pool table rose to palpable levels. Without a word, the guys at the pool table stepped up behind Kevin.

"Where is he," asked Blue Mohawk.

"I told you, we don't serve your kind. Get out while you still can."

The taller of the two women gave our table a long, last look. "We were misinformed. Come on, Joyce. Let's go."

Without another word, the two women slipped out the front door. Belinda burst into tears and ran into the kitchen. Kevin shook himself, then picked up the bat and followed Belinda through the swinging doors. The were-guys went back to the pool table. A Tom Waits tune blared out from the jukebox and the sound levels returned to normal.

"What was that all about?" I asked, to no one in particular.

Herman shushed me. "Penfield witches."

Lou's seat beside me was empty. I hadn't even noticed he'd gone Guess he wasn't kidding about staying away from witches.

Even after the women left, the atmosphere in the pub remained unsettled. The party broke up soon after. Humans and vamps alike drifted off. Rhys and I lingered in the parking lot to say our goodbyes to Henri and the rest of the band.

"I'm going to miss you," I said. In some ways, Henri knew me better than Rhys did. More than anything I wanted to tell him to stay, but Rhys was right. For the first time in his immortality, Henri was free to make his own choices. For good or bad, he had that right.

Henri hugged me tight. "Don't worry. March will be here before you know it, and I expect Blix to be talking by then. You've got to make him part of your life, Mattie. He could save your life one day, if you let him."

"I will. I promise."

Rhys and I hung around until Juno and Henri drove off in the band bus, with the roadies in the van behind them.

He slipped his arms around me. "Don't worry, he'll be fine." He kissed my forehead. "And so will you."

We waited at the side of the road for a break in the

traffic before crossing to Rhys's truck.

"Mattie, wait up a sec!" Lou called out from behind us. He trotted across the highway toward us.

The limo came out of nowhere. Low and lean, like a great white shark, it plowed into Lou without hesitation. He flew over the hood and hit the windshield. The limo squealed to a stop, backed up and there was a ghastly double thud as Lou fell to the pavement and went under the wheels. The car took off like a bat out of hell.

Lou lay in a crumpled heap by the side of the road less than ten feet from us. I ran to him, ignoring the angry protest of blaring car horns. Cars screeched to a halt or swerved abruptly around us.

Lou was on his side, his breath coming in labored gasps. I checked his carotid pulse and felt a thready heartbeat. "Please, just hang in there, for me okay?"

"The ambulance is on their way," Rhys said. "I'm going to move the truck." Moments later, Rhys had his truck in position, blinkers flashing—a barrier protecting Lou from the oncoming traffic.

"Stay with me, Lou," I murmured.

Lou let out a low moan. "Ribs busted," he grunted. "Felt 'em go."

"You're going to be fine." I said it as much for myself as for Lou, and I prayed it was true.

"That was no accident." His cheek was a bloody pulp of road burn.

"We'll find this guy and make him pay. I swear it," I promised. I smoothed his hair out of his eyes, blinking back angry tears.

"No. Listen," he gasped. He squinted in the glare of the truck's headlights.

"Don't you die on me, Lou! Don't you even think about it." In the distance I heard a siren whine.

"Those women," he grunted. "They were looking for me." He opened his fist. A blackened and battered coin lay in his palm. It was surrounded by a golden aura. "Take it. Keep it with you"

The coin gleamed brighter when I touched it.

He winced. "Ah, crap. I was afraid of that."

"What is it?" The ambulance squealed to a stop behind Rhys's truck, lights flashing.

"Detects black magic. We've been cursed."

CHAPTER 7

BY THE TIME the EMTs loaded him into the ambulance, Lou was unconscious. The sheriff's deputy arrived at the same time. We had to wait until he took statements from all the witnesses—more than a dozen of us. We all said pretty much the same thing—the limo had come out of nowhere. It happened so fast, no one got a license plate number on the vehicle, but hey, how many white stretch limos could there be in Penfield?

"It's not the limo I'm worried about," said the deputy. "It's probably stolen. The driver has probably dumped it already. We'll find it in a couple of days—in a barn or a canal somewhere, stripped for parts. Unless we catch them in the vehicle, finding the driver is going to be tough."

Kevin, the bartender, described the two women

who'd come into the bar. "It was those witches, dammit. They said they were looking for someone, but I wasn't having any of it. I told them to clear out."

"Do you know them?"

"No, but they all have a distinctive smell. These two reeked of it. Set the whole bar on edge."

The deputy paled when he realized he was speaking to a were-guy. To his credit, he kept on going.

"Who were they looking for?"

"They didn't mention any names, and I didn't ask." Kevin answered, with more than a little heat.

The deputy took careful notes of everything the witnesses said, except the part about the witches. He addressed the crowd of witnesses. "Anyone recognize these ah, women?"

No one said a word.

"Anyone know of any connections between the victim and these women?"

Again, silence from the crowd.

I slipped my hand into my jacket pocket, feeling for the coin Lou had given me for safekeeping. He wanted me to have it—I wasn't about to hand it over.

After making sure he had all our contact information, the deputy told us we were free to go.

I managed to maintain my cool until Rhys started up the truck. "Did you notice Deputy Weber's eyes glaze over when Kevin mentioned the witches?"

"Aye. But to be fair, most of the witnesses were all werewolves and vampires. He might have been a bit overwhelmed."

"Maybe," I admitted. "Lou says the sheriff's department has a hands-off stance when it comes to the Penfield witches. He says they're a cult. I'll bet no one lifts a finger to find out who did this."

"That's why the paranormal community has to stick together. I think it's great that you and Lou have teamed up."

It wasn't the first time I'd heard Rhys say that. We pulled into the hospital parking lot. "Yeah, but it's not right. Lou said those women in Growlers were looking for us." I showed Rhys the glowing coin that Lou had given me. As soon as I dropped it into Rhys's hand, it turned dark.

"Interesting." Rhys switched on the cab light to examine the bit of blackened metal more closely. He turned it over in his palm. "It's a coin, all right. Silver. Couple thousand years old, I'd guess. I'd need to examine it under magnification to be sure."

He held it out to me,

At my touch, the glow returned. "Lou said it detects the presence of black magic." I shoved the coin into the pocket of my jeans. "What do you know about curses?"

"That's not really my area of study. I've run into more than a few artifacts that were said to have been cursed or blessed in some way. I suspect a lot of them were fakes."

"What about witches?

"I've been accused of being a witch myself more than once. It's just a label, Mattie. Times past, any female healer, even a midwife, could be considered a witch. I don't have much experience with modern witches. What many would describe as black magic is merely the aspects of focused power used for unnatural purposes. Humans have always been fascinated by the occult."

I wanted to ask him more, but we'd reached the waiting area. Honey Briscoe was there, sitting alone on one of the orange leatherette couches. Her eyes were red and puffy.

I sat beside her. "What happened? Is it one of the boys?"

She shook her head. "No, they're fine. It's Lou--."

"Yeah, we know." I put my arm around her. We saw it happen."

Rhys took a chair opposite. "Is he going to be okay?"

"You just missed the surgeon." She began. "He said Lou's got head trauma with brain swelling, a badly broken leg, crushed ribs, and who knows what else. He's in bad shape. They've put him in an induced coma until the swelling comes down," Her lovely brown eyes filled with tears. "I couldn't believe it when they called me. It was like Nate all over again."

She blew her nose on a crumpled tissue. "He is the boy's godfather and he's got no one else. I'm listed as his next of kin. They said he'd been hit by a car?"

We told her about the hit and run. I didn't mention the witches or the coin or the curse thing. No point in making things worse. Rhys caught my eye and I knew he agreed with me.

But Honey wasn't fooled. "Growlers Pub? That's in Penfield. What was he doing over there?"

Rhys explained about Henri's going away party.

She made a face. "Well, Growlers *is* neutral ground. But Penfield isn't safe for him."

"Why, what's wrong with Penfield?"

"There's a coven there—a cult, really. They used to be called the Penfield witches, but that's misnomer. The sorcerer who leads it now is obsessed with the dark arts and arcane knowledge. They're not above using physical violence to get what they want. They've sworn to kill Lou if he ever sets foot in Penfield again"

"Kevin told the deputy it was witches," Rhys said.

She shot him a cynical look. "That won't matter.

They've got people on the sheriff's payroll who will make sure that the witness statements get misplaced or misfiled or trashed. It happens all the time. They're evil and know perfectly well that no one dares to stop them.

Rhys and I exchanged a glance. "You really think the Penfield witches that did this," I said, softly.

She clenched her fists. "Don't call them witches! It's an insult to--." Her shoulders slumped. "I'm sorry. I shouldn't have said that. Call them whatever you like." She sighed. "It's been a long day and I need to get home to my boys. I can let you know if Lou's condition changes." She picked up her purse and stood to leave.

Rhys and I walked her out to the parking lot and made sure she got to her car.

"It's not right." I climbed into the truck and scooted over to sit next to Rhys. "Honey knows the sheriff isn't going to do anything to find that limo driver. I'm going to find out who did this, and make sure Sheriff Reynolds does his job. He likes, me, Rhys. I know he does. He'll listen to me."

Rhys drove through the quiet streets of Shore Haven. Not even the bars were open at this hour. "This could be a real can of worms. If Frank were still around, I'd say we talk to him, but I don't feel the same way about the new guy." Agent Frank Porter had been the FBI's local supernatural investigator until last year, when he took a new assignment in New Orleans. Rhys and Frank had been partners in a lot of special investigations that weren't necessarily within the purview of the FBI's authority. They trusted each other.

"Ted Roper," I prompted. Frank had been a lot more approachable than Roper, who seemed more of a by-the-book kind of guy. "The only time I asked him for help, he made me feel like an idiot."

Rhys parked the truck in front of the big old Queen Anne. Tonight was supposed to be our first night alone in the house. "What are you talking about? He saved your life in that fire." He ran his hand over my still-short hair and helped me out of the truck.

"That's not what I meant." We walked up the path to the front porch. A sudden swarm of will-o-the-wisps filled the air, like a cloud above our heads. They completely surrounded us—dozens of them, swirling around our heads, pinging off our hair and clothes like demonic fireflies. In the quiet calm of the night air, I could hear them whisper:

Loosa, loosa, loose...Loosa, loosa, loose!

I grinned at Rhys, who looked just as astonished as I felt. "Can you hear them?"

He cocked his head for a moment. "Nope. I got nothing." He shook his head.

"This is what happened to Charlie and me a while back," I said. The lights bombarded us for another few moments, then, as suddenly as they'd appeared, they were gone.

"That was pretty cool," he admitted. "I've never known fairy fire to behave like that. What did they say?"

I unlocked the door and stepped inside. "Same as before. It sounds like, 'loosa loose'. Charlie thinks it's a warning."

Rhys took my jacket and hung it up next to his on the coat rack. The house seemed to echo in Henri's absence. "Some folks believe they're messengers of an impending death.

My throat went dry. "You think Lou is going to die?"

He caressed my cheek. "No, I meant that it's a Senequois legend. Honey could tell you more."

I led the way upstairs to my room. "Honey Briscoe?"

"Yeah. Her grandmother was a storyteller. Honey knows all the old stories. Maybe she knows about the Loosa thing."

Rhys wrapped me in his arms. For awhile, my thoughts were focused on delving into the deeper territories of intimacy and naked delight that we shared whenever we were alone together. And snuggling up together on a chilly night after such a grueling day wasn't bad, either.

But even with Rhys sleeping peacefully beside me, I couldn't relax. Every time I closed my eyes, I saw Lou crumpled beneath the wheels of that limo. He was a good man. How could someone have purposely run him down like that?

I hated bullies. So what if Lou and I had found out where they held their rituals? No reason to hex him, or whatever they'd done to us. Or run him down like that. The more I thought about it, the more convinced I became that the deputy who had taken our statements tonight didn't believe any of the Growlers witnesses. Lou didn't deserve this. At the very least, law enforcement should be looking after their own. The deputy acted like he didn't care whether they found the driver or not.

But I did. I made a silent promise to Lou that I would find out who had done this horrible thing to him and bring them to justice. There had to be a way to find this guy. I picked up the coin Lou had given me from the bedside table. It glowed in the dark room like a beacon. I wondered if the black magic it detected in me was Morta's, or if Lou had been right about the curse.

What did it mean?

I had an uneasy feeling that if Lou was right, I was about to find out.

CHAPTER 8

ALL DAY AT work, my mind kept wandering. I couldn't stop thinking about Lou. Sheriff Reynolds wouldn't do anything. The coin Lou had given me was dimmer today, but stilled flared whenever I picked it up. If there really was a dark sorcerer operating a cult in Monroe County, maybe there was something the FBI could do. The only person I knew in the local field office was Ted Roper, so I called him and asked him to meet me for lunch.

I figured it might be better to speak to him informally, so I suggested Rudy's Red Hots, a lunch-wagon vendor who worked just a block from the FBI offices in downtown Rochester. The good weather was still holding, so we ate outside at the mini-tables Rudy had set up for his customers.

Both of us were on our lunch hour, so there wasn't a lot of time for chit-chat. I got directly to the point. "What is the FBI's position on witchcraft?"

Roper shrugged and took a sip of his soda. "In the '80s, the Supreme Court ruled that Witchcraft is a legitimate religion. People who practice witchcraft as a religion are entitled to the same rights and constitutional protections as followers of any other recognized belief system. I'm guessing that's not what you wanted to know, is it?"

"Rats. No, not really." I tried again. "What is the FBI's supernatural taskforce stance on witchcraft? I know you guys hunt down, um, unlicensed demon masters, but what about Sorcerers? Black magic, that kind of thing." Being an unlicensed demon master myself, I could end up in a whole lot of trouble if Roper ever found out about Blix.

He put down his half-eaten hot dog. "Not really a lunch topic, but okay. Some people try to claim their criminal activity is actually part of their religious practice. But criminal acts, such as human sacrifice, are not recognized as part of any religious practice. Murder, extortion, theft; these are all crimes, regardless of the killer's religious affiliation or purpose. Just to be clear, the FBI is interested in the apprehension of criminals and the prosecution of criminal acts and criminal organizations, not the persecution of personal religious beliefs or religions."

"What about sorcery? Satanic cults?"

He gave me a hard look. "Why don't you just tell me what you want to know, Mattie?"

I explained how Lou Scali had been run down by a hit and run driver. "Everyone keeps telling me that Sheriff Reynolds won't touch a case involving witchcraft."

"A hit and run is outside FBI jurisdiction. Even if it was attempted murder, it's not something we would get called in on."

"Suppose it was the member of a witch cult who was driving? People are afraid of the Penfield witches. Lou Scali and I saw them performing a ritual last week. And now Lou is in a coma and no one is going to do anything about it."

"What kind of ritual? Did you observe any criminal activity?"

"No." I could see where this was going. "Lou said it was some kind of preparation for something bigger. Layering, he called it. Someone saw us when we were leaving."

"Where was this ritual performed?"

"It didn't exactly have an address. It was dark, and we hiked in. I could find it, though."

"Private property? "

I remembered the bullet-pocked signs posted around the barn and fences. I sighed. "Yeah, probably. Look I know what you're going to say--."

"Damn right. You were trespassing."

"Sheesh." I chugged the last of my iced tea and chucked the remains of my lunch into the nearest trash bin. "I should have known better. Forget it."

If I wanted action, I was going to have to do it myself. Dollars to donuts that private investigator book Lou had given me would have the answers I was looking for. This was the last time I'd ever ask for Roper's help.

"It's nothing personal. I'm just doing my job." Roper wadded up his trash and disposed of it as well. "Let me do a little research on the cult and sorcery angle. I'll get back to you."

"Thanks," I said, but I didn't plan on holding my breath waiting for him. I should have known I couldn't count on him. Unlike his predecessor, Roper's stint as a supernatural investigator wasn't a personal calling; it was just another step on the ladder.

Four months ago, when he'd arrived in Rochester with his demon-sniffing dog, every alternate individual in town had been terrified they'd be exposed as non—human. He probably expected to eliminate the demon problem and get a big promotion. Roper pooh-poohed my reports of dream spiders, only to see me go up against an angry six-foot tall female and her hatchlings. Sure, he'd dragged me out of the flames and saved my life, but not before I'd saved a dozen innocent teenagers. He'd accomplished exactly nothing since he'd arrived here. And now he was acting as if he was doing me a favor. I would have respected him more if he'd just said *fuggedaboutit*.

Fool me twice, shame on me. Next time, well, there just wouldn't be a next time.

After my shift, I headed over to the hospital to check on Lou.

I met Honey as she was coming out of the building. "You can't see him," she told me. "He's still in a coma. They're saying it's a miracle that he lasted through the night. I still don't understand why they went after him like that. Why?"

I swallowed the hard lump of emotion which had welled up in my throat. Lou couldn't die. He just couldn't.

Honey looked terrible. Dark circles ringed her eyes; her beautiful caramel skin looked sallow. I felt bad for her. I told her about working a stakeout with Lou. "We followed the husband to a cemetery in Penfield. We found the coven performing a layering ritual. Once he realized who they were, Lou got me out of there pretty fast, but one of them saw us as we were leaving. They probably tracked him through the license plate on his car. And last night, two women came into the bar, looking for someone, but they didn't say who. It must have been Lou."

"Oh God." She closed her eyes. "I thought this was over." Her body swayed.

I thought she was going to faint. I helped her down the steps and we sat on a warm bench in the dappled shade of a scarlet maple.

"I guess I just wanted it to be." She chewed her lower lip. "I can't tell you how sorry I am that you've been dragged into this, Mattie."

"Dragged into what, exactly? I'm not even sure what's going on. Until last week, I'd never heard of the Penfield witch—um, cult."

"No reason you should have. Ten years ago, before the FBI had a supernatural bureau, Nate and Lou were investigating the disappearance of a Picston City employee. As they tracked down leads in the case, they discovered other disappearances as well. They became convinced that someone was targeting long-time members of the Penfield coven. They were close to an arrest when Nate was killed."

"I remember that," I said. "Nate took a bullet meant for Lou."

She shook her head, her lips pressed into a thin line. "That was the official story, but not what happened. Nate was poisoned."

My mouth went dry. "What? How?"

"With water hemlock. Common as a weed, and one of the deadliest plants in North America. Almost a cliché, in terms of a witch's weapon, wouldn't you say?" She gave me a bitter smile. "Someone mixed it into their lunch salads. The investigators never discovered who was responsible, and no one was ever prosecuted. The department hushed it up. Gave Nate a medal for bravery. Of course Lou blamed himself, but there was no black magic involved. Neither of them ever suspected there was anything wrong with their food."

"How awful. I'm sorry."

"That wasn't the end of it. Once or twice a year, someone leaves little carved wooden figures on our porches, covered in blood. It's a form of intimidation, meant to keep us off balance. I won't let the boys answer the door when I'm not home. Last week, a swarm of swamp lights appeared in Lou's living room."

"Excuse me?"

"Swamp lights. That's what we called them when I was a kid. Or fey lights. White people call them will-o-the-wisps. Lou said they weren't evil, just the cult playing head games, but now I'm not so sure."

I slumped back against the bench. "Charlie and I had a similar experience," I said. "He was pretty sure they were bad news."

"When I was little, my grandmother told me that swamp lights are lost spirits, unable to pass beyond the veil. They serve as messengers between the land of the living and the dead. It is said that their message can only be heard by the intended recipient. Charlie's suggestion that it's a warning could also be correct."

"They kept saying loosa-loosa."

Honey gave me a worried look. "Sorry, I never learned many Senequois words, but Charlie speaks the language. Maybe he could tell you." She rubbed her face. "I thought the nightmare was over years ago. That cult is a cancer. Now Lou is going to die and it's all my fault."

Instinctively, I put my arm around her. "You haven't done anything wrong."

She stiffened, her expression stony. "You have no idea what you're saying."

"No. Lou told me. The Penfield witch cult did this. They killed Nate and tried to kill Lou. They're the ones who cursed Lou and me."

She wrapped her arms around herself and stared at her shoes. "They won't give up. It's personal for them. They won't ever stop until they kill me and my kids."

I understood survivor's guilt—I'd dealt with it nearly all my life. I couldn't imagine how hard her life must've been—raising two kids on her own. She looked so forlorn.

"Honey, it's not true. You had nothing to do with any of this."

"Oh yes I do," she said, her voice thick with emotion. She raised her worried brown eyes to mine. "I'm one of them. I'm a Penfield witch."

CHAPTER 9

"YOU HAVE TO understand," Honey explained. "That the history of the Penfield witches began in the 18th century, when the first settlers moved into the area now known as Penfield. The Senequois people, my ancestors, welcomed their new neighbors and helped them establish their homesteads. The Senequois tribeswomen in particular embraced the newly arrived white settler women as distant kin, and took it upon themselves to teach them about the local plants, medicinal herbs, and wildcrafting.

"Some of the women of my line became very close to several of the wives of the first settlers, or so the story has been passed down to me. They met regularly to share their knowledge. As it happened, the white women who were most accepting of the Senequois were not particular about attending church services every week. As the women learned herb lore and healing from their Senequois sisters, their children survived in greater numbers. Their husband's crops and animals flourished. Their farms prospered. They were not plagued by pestilence and disease as severely as those on other farms. As sometimes happens, others in the community began to notice that these white women had become suspiciously friendly with the native tribeswomen.

"Fueled by jealousy and ignorance, rumors began to circulate that some of these settler women were witches. The wives of the more prosperous of these homesteaders became known as the Penfield witches. The name stuck.

"Senequois women have always shared their knowledge of wildcraft. We never excluded anyone who sought to learn from us. I grew up believing that the way of the People was one of peace and enlightenment. I was fourteen when I joined the circle, and we were known as the Penfield Eight for many, many years. By that time, only two of us could claim Senequois ancestry—my grandmother and me."

A woman with two small children passed us, and Honey waited until they were out of earshot. She kept her voice low.

"Then, ten years ago, a brother and sister asked to join our circle. They were European—new to the area, and knowledgeable herbalists. They were so enthusiastic and eager to learn. They opened their home to the circle for our meetings and their drying shed for our herbs. They were British; unfamiliar with the ancient myths and folklore of the Senequois people. My grandmother, a storyteller of our clan, was flattered; and it was wonderful to hear the old stories again. Everyone loved this new energy coming into the group. John and Liddy had some different ideas and invited new members into our little circle. As our membership swelled, the focus of our circle began to change.

"John and Liddy were psychics, they told us— each of them gifted with the ability to communicate with the spirit world. Jonathan in particular, claimed the ability to summon certain spirits for the purpose of gaining knowledge. He was both charming persuasive, and before long, had convinced nearly everyone in the circle that the pursuit of arcane knowledge was a far nobler pursuit than messing about with weeds and seeds, as he called it. He said he could perform miracles with the power of a full and proper coven united behind him.

"It all happened so gradually, even my

grandmother was convinced. He became our leader, or high priest, as he preferred we call him. It was just a name, and I went along with it like everyone else in the circle. His sister Liddy became our high priestess. The day came when John and Liddy presented each of us with a hooded black robe. That was the day I told Nate I was one of the Penfield Eight and I wanted out.

"I was pregnant with Arby, and Nate Junior was about to start kindergarten. Moving closer to Nate's job in Picston made a lot of sense. Nate's partner Lou owned a duplex and his tenants were moving out. It was the perfect setup for us.

"Jonathan didn't like it one bit. At first, he tried to persuade Nate and me to move into his big house with his sister Liddy."

"Wait," I said. Are you talking about John and Liddy Fewkes? As in the puppet lady?"

She nodded. "Yes. Back then, they lived in a big old farmhouse in Penfield. They had more room than they needed, he said. He offered to let us live with them— rent free. He'd already persuaded my grandmother to move in with them. We'd be a big happy family. Of course Nate and I had no intention of doing that. We told him about the baby and how Nate Junior would be able to walk to kindergarten. We tried to be diplomatic.

"Liddy took a different approach. She tried to convince me that Nate was cheating on me. She even implied that he'd propositioned her. She told me he would break my heart and leave me for another woman. I'd have to raise his kids all alone. She kept at it."

"What a horrible thing to say."

Honey smoothed her skirt. "Of course, I didn't believe a word of it. Lydia could be rather dramatic at times. But the pregnancy had me feeling vulnerable, and she got some of the other women in the circle to hint at the same sort of thing. I'd known some of these women a long time. I trusted them. They'd become convinced that John and Liddy were going to bring real magic into the circle, and Nate's job with the police department made John and Liddy uneasy. John said that Nate had a negative attitude that constricted the natural flow of true power, whatever that meant. They even got my grandmother to suggest that I divorce Nate, saying that the life of my unborn child was at risk, and that the sisterhood of the coven took care of their own.

"When I didn't back down, John reacted badly. It was crazy, but he acted as if I *belonged* to him. Like I was his property and that my leaving was some kind of personal betrayal. I thought he was acting like a spoilt child, but I had no idea that this was just the beginning.

"On the day we moved, Jonathan and his sister brought the rest of the coven over to our apartment in Penfield and made a big scene. Like a protest, with a bullhorn and everything. He told us he'd already cursed Lou and this was our last chance. Somehow, he'd convinced everyone in the coven to support him on this—even my grandmother!

"Nate was furious and I was embarrassed and angry—and more than a little freaked out. Nate called in the sheriff—this was before Jim Reynolds was elected. Sheriff Bland refused to come, saying that Jonathan and his supporters had a right to free speech. They weren't breaking any laws.

"Then my ninety-three year-old grandmother, who had never been sick a day in her life, died in her sleep three weeks after we moved. There was nothing inherently suspicious about her death, but it seemed too coincidental. I couldn't get it out of my head. Then her body was 'accidently' cremated, against her explicit wishes, so that she did not receive the traditional Senequois blessings and ceremony of the dead. You must understand that for a Senequois, the ceremony of the dead, in addition to being a fundamental part of our culture, protects the soul of the departed until it reaches the afterlife. I told Nate I was scared.

"Two weeks after my grandmother's death, Nate was dead." She blinked away tears. "Baby Ray was born a month after he died. Everything went quiet then. Lou took care of me and the boys. We waited for them to do something. Lydia had the nerve to tell me about her prediction of Nate's impending death had been correct. She and John expected me to come crawling back, but Lou was my rock. Every time we started to relax, another bloody warning showed up on the porch."

"A few years ago, I saw John and Liddy at Wegmans. They acted as if nothing had happened. Just seeing them made me sick to my stomach. They told me they were planning to open a shop in Shore Haven. We'd be neighbors, just like old times. The way they looked at me--." Honey shivered.

"I was terrified. I couldn't stand the idea of living in the same town with the people responsible for killing Nate and my grandmother. Lou assured me that they were just playing head games. He swore he'd keep me and the boys safe. He checked around and found out the bank had foreclosed on their house. The shop in Shore Haven is a lease. They're in financial trouble. They haven't been in any position to start anything."

She blew her nose. "Then last year, Liddy started

putting on those stupid puppet shows. I feel like a monster forbidding Arby to watch them, but I don't want Liddy to get her claws into my kids."

"After all this time? I don't get it. What's the point?"

"John is a sociopath. His sister Liddy is even worse. They'd use anyone and do anything to get what they want, Mattie. Intimidation and black magic are their tools of choice. Be glad you don't know them. Stay away from them.

The next day, I was sitting astride the Vic, idling at the stoplight light in front of Killer Dave's, when a movement across the street caught my eye. It was Liddy Fewkes, leaving the flower shop. Her car was parked out front, and she got in.

An impatient driver in the car behind me honked, informing me the light had changed to green. On impulse, I whipped into the empty lot behind Dave's. I peeked around the corner of the restaurant in time to see Liddy drive off.

I debated going in. In spite of what Honey had said about them, I couldn't help but think that maybe her memories from ten years earlier were a little overblown. And I was curious. After what she'd told me, I thought maybe I hadn't imagined Liddy's doll speaking to me at career day. What if there were more dolls in the shop? I'd love to see if Lou's coin reacted to them. With Liddy gone, John would be there by himself, and he wouldn't know me from Adam.

I thought about summoning Blix but decided against it. If John Fewkes was as powerful a sorcerer as Lou and Honey seemed to think, he might be able to sense my djemon's presence. Besides, it was broad daylight. As far as anyone knew, I was just another customer.

Five minutes. What would it hurt?

A bell over the door tinkled as I stepped inside. The shop was cluttered and crowded with antiques; the pungent scent of tea and dried herbs was strong, but not unpleasant.

A man stepped out from behind a striped curtain behind the counter, and I got my first look at John Fewkes. Tall, balding, with a walrus moustache and a ruddy complexion. He wore a black pinstriped suit, with a black shirt and silver tie—expensive-looking and veddy proper. This was the high priest of the Penfield witch cult? He looked more like a banker than a sorcerer.

"What can I help you with today, Madame?"

His voice filled the small shop—rich and deep. Both of them were actors, I remembered. That, I believed. Although, come to think of it, Liddy did not have an accent. One of them must be faking it.

"Just browsing," I glanced around the cramped shop. "Ah, where are the herbs?"

He smirked. "Weeds and seeds in the back," he declared. "My sister just stepped out. If you require assistance, you'd best wait until she returns."

Something about him struck me as familiar, but I could not figure it out.

I wound my way through narrow, twisting aisles of mirrored armoires, ornately carved benches; dressers piled high with crockery and decorative glassware. A collection of life-sized antique carousel animals led the way to the tea room. Inside, two small tables and a loveseat flanked an authentic-looking saloon bar, sans the bar stools. Brass lamps with stained glass shades gave the room a warm and cheerful glow. Ruffled chintz curtains matched the tablecloths and cushions on the window seat. Instead of a mirror, the back wall was filled with glass-fronted cabinets containing assorted herbs, dried flowers, ribbons, and large glass canisters of loose tea.

And dolls.

A floor to ceiling cabinet, nearly six feet wide, was

devoted to antique wooden dolls and marionettes. I approached the cabinet, looking for the doll I remembered, but I didn't see it. The cabinet was locked. I held Lou's coin against the glass, and my palm as well, but whether the glass kept me from sensing trapped spirits within the dolls, or whether these dolls were nothing special, I couldn't tell.

I scanned the cluttered room, searching for the slightest indication that this was some sort of witch lair. The tearoom was charming, in a cliché sort of way. Nothing remotely satanic or cultish here. Maybe they kept that stuff hidden. I don't know what I expected, but I felt sort of disappointed by the place.

There was a stairwell leading up to the second floor. Tempting, but probably locked, and I didn't have enough nerve to try the stairs. They probably creaked.

I made my way back to the front of the shop. Fewkes had a copy of the London Times spread across the counter before him. He didn't look the least bit dangerous.

Something drew me closer. Like a riddle that needed to be answered, I just had to know more. I approached the counter, Lou's coin hidden in my hand. "This place is charming," I nodded at the paper he was reading. "Anything interesting?"

He looked at me over the top of his half-glasses.

"Art thou base, common, and popular?" Something flickered in John's Fewkes's eyes, sending a chill right through me. That look told me he'd seen something in me, and was trying to puzzle me out as well.

I frowned, uncertain whether I'd been insulted. *Probably.* "Excuse me?"

He closed the newspaper and folded it. "Shakespeare. Henry the Fifth. A carriage clock on the shelf behind him began to chime softly. "It is closing time, Madame, and I have an appointment. As much as I should like to continue this sparkling conversation, I cannot." Sarcasm dripped from every word. He stepped out from behind the counter and waved me toward the door.

I suddenly remembered why he sounded so familiar. It wasn't the accent—it was the attitude. My gut told me that John Fewkes must be, had to be, Zeypax's master. Rhys and Henri had told me repeatedly that djemons took on the same characteristics as their masters. The djemon I'd banished from that old farmhouse had the same arrogant manner.

"Okay, thanks," I mumbled and slipped out of the shop. I heard him chuckle as I shut the door behind me.

I couldn't shake the feeling that I'd just made a huge mistake.

Blix was waiting for me when I got home. He bounced up and down on the dining room table, squeaking like a windup toy. I dumped my helmet and jacket on the floor and hurried over to see what the commotion was all about. I thought he wanted to show me something on his Read and Spell tablet. Ever since I'd given it to him, he'd been glued to it and happily preoccupied for days at a time.

Instead, he clutched my cell phone in his delicate black claws.

Oh jeeze. He probably thought it was just another version of his Speak and Read tool. I should have told him not to touch it. Now, it was too late. Say goodbye to my contact list.

"Hand it over, Blix."

He held it up to me, his yellow eyes dilated. His blue tongue flicked in and out uncertainly.

I took the phone and he scampered up my arm to sit in the crook of my elbow. I scrolled through my contact list, but Blix's nimble fingers beat me to the punch.

All I could do was stare in amazement. He'd updated every single entry in my phone list, and somehow managed to find out their complete contact information, including address, phone and email, and categorized them as to Picston, friends, and family. In some cases, there were even satellite photos of the buildings where they lived. Even a new address and phone number for my brother Lance in South Carolina—and I hadn't heard from him in months.

"Hey!" I'd never bothered to fill in anything more than just the barest phone number or email of any particular contact. Blix had found links for some of them—to websites and network connections.

"Good boy--." I said, and then quickly corrected myself. Rhys had been coaching me in the correct way to speak to and behave toward a djemon. "You have done well, Blix."

The little djemon positively beamed at my properly-worded praise. He leapt to the table and stamped his little feet as if to say, follow me!

"What?"

He scampered into the parlor, where Madame Coumlie's personal computer sat, unused since Henri left because I'd forgotten to ask him for the password.

But that hadn't stopped Blix. He seated himself on the desk in front of the keyboard and entered a password, then began to manipulate the mouse, selecting the file he was looking for. He opened a spreadsheet and then a text file. His fingers fairly flew over the keys, his nails making little clicking noises against the keys as he typed.

It was Madam Coumlie's client list, something Henri and I had been meaning to get to, but hadn't. There were hundreds of names and email addresses here. All in alphabetical order. "Excellent work, Blix."

He opened yet another file, which had links to all of the various media accounts of Lou's hit and run accident. And somehow, he'd managed to hack into the hospital's database and upload the file of Lou's medical records. There was even a file folder with newspaper reports on the death of Lou's former partner, Nate Briscoe, a decade earlier.

"Holy crap." I sank into the desk chair, intrigued. In the final file was a profile piece dated yesterday. An interview with Sheriff Reynolds. When asked about the hit-and-run accident in Penfield, Reynolds had declined to comment. *Investigation continuing*. Right.

"Good heavens, Blix, well done!" I couldn't believe he'd accomplished so much. My mind raced at the possibilities.

"Can you speak, Blix? Say something."

His entire body slumped. He emitted a sound that was part gurgle, part whine, part chirp. He looked miserable.

My first instinct was to pick him up and rub his belly, but I caught myself. Instead I ignored his failed attempt and gave him something else I was certain he could do.

"Well, keep working on it. In the meantime, I want you to find out everything you can about the Penfield witches, er, cult. I want to see anything you can find. Especially any newspaper articles, clippings, or photos. I want to know who they are, and whether there have been any charges filed against them in the past." I thought for a moment. "And while you're at it, see what you can find out about witchcraft in general. And spell layering. And occultists. I want to know about them, too. And while you're at it, see what else you can find on Nate Briscoe's murder."

Blix quivered with excitement and began to tap at the keyboard.

Gee, I'd never had an assistant before. This could work.

CHAPTER 10

MASTER FOO HAD me using a bamboo pole for my Qhua Bei practice—my first weapon. It wasn't a blade, but at least I was making progress. I soon discovered that the pole, as light as it was, got heavier with every minute of practice. In Qhua Bei, the movements must be precise, and as I struggled to keep my arms and elbows up, my footwork deteriorated.

But when I practiced my Qhua Bei movements to Mr. Maestro's dance mix, everything changed. The music seemed to awaken energy reserves I didn't know I possessed. The urge to move to the music was irresistible—and the footwork Mr. Maestro had taught us translated well into the movements of Qhua Bei. Moreover, the music made my solitary practice not so deadly dull. Actually, I'd gotten the idea from Henri, who always practiced to the sound of his beloved Wiley Willy and the Rogues album.

I brought Mr. Maestro's dance mix CD along when Rhys and I went to Master Foo's practice on Saturday morning. As usual, the Master observed my practice without comment I gave myself over to the music and it moved though me, guiding my movements. I didn't even have to think about it. The backbeat gave me confidence in my footwork and every movement of my body felt natural. It was a great workout, and I was breathing hard when I finished. But for once, my arms and legs weren't trembling with fatigue.

Master Foo nodded, his expression every bit as dour as usual. I didn't care. I was onto something here, and this was the best practice I'd ever done for him.

But instead of telling me what to work on, he beckoned me out into the practice yard. "Bring the music with you, Missy."

I followed him out to the practice ring where Rhys was doing his warm-up. I set the boom box on the ringside table.

"You two together," Master Foo said. He positioned Rhys and I so that we were standing back-to-back, each in our 'ready' position—Rhys in a two-handed grip on his sword, and me with my skinny green bamboo pole.

Rhys caught my eye over his shoulder and gave

me a little wink. I'd convinced him to give it a try the previous night and we already knew what was coming. Rhys been practicing in silence for centuries, but he liked Mr. Maestro's music—and it was a whole lot better than what Henri listened to. It hadn't started as foreplay, but--.

Master Foo hit the PLAY button on the boom box and the sounds of Cab Calloway's intro to *Hi De Ho* filled the air.

Rhys and I moved through our exercises together, and the connection between us snapped into place again, just as it had the night before. It was like we shared the same mind and body. We turned together, step for step, and moved away—separate, yet undeniably connected. I could hardly believe it—for the first time ever, I was actually practicing martial arts with my boyfriend! Every time we happened to face each other, his eyes held mine and I couldn't stop grinning.

The music shifted to a Stray Cats tune, and the spark between us grew—we were in perfect sync. Rhys's feet hit the ground exactly the same time as mine. Even though I'd already gone through my entire practice for Master Foo, the music sent new energy to my tired muscles. The weight of the bamboo pole grew feather-light. I felt sexy, dangerous, and powerful. Rhys looked good enough to eat.

We were both sweat-soaked and grinning like a pair of love-struck fools when Master Foo turned off the music. Rhys grabbed my hand and kissed it; the look in his eyes telling me that if not for Master Foo's presence, we'd already be naked.

"Much better. You understand now, Missy." Master Foo gave me one of his rare smiles. His whole face crinkled up with it. "You have learned."

"This was all Mattie's idea," said Rhys. He draped his arm across my shoulders. "She's a warrior at heart. I wish I'd learned this sooner."

Master Foo gave me a small bow. "The warrior has always been within you, Missy. Today is but the first step."

Praise from Master Foo was a new experience for me. I didn't even mind the embarrassment. "The dance lessons helped."

Master Foo pointed at me. "The music teaches the student what this Master could not. Mind, body, and spirit are one. With practice, you shall learn to do it naturally, so that you can call it to you whenever you need it. You felt the connection today, yes?"

"Yes," I glanced at Rhys. "It gets better every time."

"Trust is the key," Master Foo said. "In battle, a trained warrior acts on instinct."

His rare praise had me beaming.

On the short walk home after practice, Rhys and I walked arm in arm—like an old married couple. As badass as Rhys looked, sometimes, he could be pretty sweet, too.

"The druids don't have much use for modern music," he said. "But the music Mr. Maestro teaches is different—primal. I feel it in my bones." We'd reached the front porch. He led me to the swing and I sat beside him. The noonday sun was warm. The sky, a brilliant turquoise. "You are that music, Mattie."

I punched him playfully. "Cut the mushy stuff. You're embarrassing me." From anyone else, I would have melted into a puddle of love right there, but this was dangerous territory. We both knew that sooner or later, this wasn't going to end well.

"You must know we're onto something really good here. I feel it when we're dancing—you're completely in the moment and everything is sure and right and I love seeing you like that. And then at other times, I feel you pulling back. Master Foo is right. Why don't you trust me?"

And there it was. Somehow it always came back to trust; or at least my inability to give it.

"Rhys, I do trust you. I asked you to move in with me."

"That's right, you did." He stood and scooped me

up into his arms. "I don't think we've properly marked the occasion yet." When he wiggled his eyebrows he looked like Groucho Marx.

I giggled. "It's not even noon." But I wrapped my arms around his neck and let him carry me upstairs.

Much later, I lay beside him, watching the shadows on the walls lengthen into late afternoon. Somehow, Rhys had become far more to me than the word boyfriend could imply. I could not imagine my life without him anymore. And I knew Rhys felt the same about me.

This was what Master Foo had been trying to teach me. We were stronger together than apart. Rhys would never willingly hurt me. Something had changed between us.

Okay, so yeah, he was immortal and I wasn't, but nobody's perfect. Every relationship had challenges, right? Why couldn't I just accept his immortality and go with the flow? Live in the moment, as Rhys so often told me.

The warm skin of his muscular back felt like velvet beneath my fingers. He stirred and rolled over to face me, and the smile in his eyes erased my doubts.

For a while.

CHAPTER 11

A WEEK PASSED, and no arrest had been made. Lou was still in intensive care, in an induced coma because of the swelling in his brain. The story hadn't even made the local news. I couldn't stand it.

After I got off work, I rode the Vic over to the Monroe County Sheriff's Department in downtown Rochester. In spite of the recent stretch of warm fall weather, October's chill came on quick after sundown. I was glad to step inside the warmth of the building.

The office closed at 5pm, but I was pretty sure Jim Reynolds would still be there. When I got off the elevator, the suite looked empty, except for the Sheriff. I could see him in his glass-walled office, working at his desk.

Jim Reynolds is a fit, good looking guy in his late

forties. He's a straight arrow, and in spite of the fact that he's arrested me more than once, I 'm pretty sure he kind of likes me.

He made a face when he saw me. "Oh no, you don't. Not another step, Blackman. Whatever it is, I want nothing to do with it. You've burned down enough buildings in this town; I don't want the Sheriff's office to be next. You're nothing but a pain in the ass, dammit."

He wouldn't say that if he meant it. "Hey, it wasn't my fault, and you know it."

"Don't give me that, I can always tell when you're lying. Besides, Roper told me you deliberately started that blaze at the amusement park."

The memory of the ballroom attic erupting in flames as the lighter ignited the spider's silk wiped the smile right off my face. I ran my hand through my still-too-short hair. "Well, okay. Yeah, I guess I did."

He waved me toward an empty chair across from his desk. "He said it was the bravest thing he'd ever seen." His glance flicked to my blackened hand. "You knew you were going to die, and you didn't hesitate. You saved those kids."

I couldn't imagine Roper saying anything of the sort. "Yeah, well, that's not why I'm here."

He glared at me over his glasses. "I'm busy,

Blackman. What do you want?"

I hesitated. Reynolds could very well kick me out of his office for asking. "I want to know what's happening with the Lou Scali hit-and-run."

He snorted. "Don't waste my time. I've got a handful of witnesses, including you, with no ID on the driver. The limo was stolen from Wayne County and hasn't been found yet. It'll probably show up in downtown Rochester, meaning it belongs to RPD. You can figure out the rest on your own. I've got other fish to fry."

Three different jurisdictions would make the case a legal nightmare. I tried to look at the case from Reynolds's standpoint. Nobody had died, and insurance would cover everything. Unless the driver turned himself in, the case was a loser. And so was Lou.

"Lou's a cop."

"Retired. Working the other side now. Chances are it was the angry ex-husband of one of his clients. I talked to him myself a few hours ago. He knows the score."

"He's awake?"

He nodded. "As of about ten this morning."

"What about the Penfield cult angle?"

He gave me a disgusted look. "I'm not even going

119

to dignify that with an answer. Every time something happens at Growlers, those were-folk blame the occultists. And every time someone trespasses on coven land, I get a call saying it's those rabid werewolves. Far as the Sheriff's Department is concerned, they're a couple of gangs who happen to share the same territory and can't get along. We're Switzerland here, unless someone comes forward with evidence I can use. If you suddenly remember the name of the limo driver who ran down Scali, I'd be happy to have one of my deputies to take your statement."

This was going to be harder than I thought. "Lou is not a were. That hit-and-run was not some neighborhood dispute. You know Lou has been on their shit list for years." I debated telling him about the ritual we'd seen, but of course he'd tell me the same thing Roper had—Lou and I had been trespassing. But I had to find a way to convince Reynolds not to quit on the case. "Maybe he saw something he wasn't supposed to see."

"Look, I have your statement. Lou's given me his—and he swears he has no idea who would want to run him down. He doesn't think he was targeted, so why would you? Unless you have new evidence, we're done. You're not one of my deputies. Hell, you're not even a private investigator. You don't belong here."

"Halloween is coming," I blurted. "They must be up to something."

"For cryin' out loud, Blackman." He rolled his eyes at me. "Halloween is their national holiday. Now get out of my office, before I arrest you for disturbing the peace." He reached into his desk drawer and pulled out an aspirin bottle.

"No, I mean, yes I know. I mean, we saw them practicing. Some kind of ritual. Out in the middle of--."

"Out." Reynolds pointed to the door.

"Okay, okay. I'm going." I knew when to back off. By the time I reached the elevator, he'd already popped a couple aspirin. He was probably just having a bad day. I knew he didn't mean anything by it.

Sheriff Reynolds likes me.

CHAPTER 12

WHEN RHYS AND I arrived at the hospital, Honey was already there, sitting in a low chair next to the bed. Lou gave us a little wave when we came in.

Lou's blackened eyes and ghastly road rash had already begun to fade. Easy to see they'd be gone in another day or two. He'd told me he was a fast healer, but it was more than that. His healing abilities were more like mine, but that didn't make what had happened to him any better. He could have been killed. It pissed me off no end that whoever had done this would probably get away with it.

"How's the leg." Rhys asked.

"No idea. I've never broken anything before. I hate being laid up like this." He patted Honey's brown hand. "Honey has offered to help me out at home until the cast comes off. The doctor says several weeks, but I sure hope not."

"The Sheriff told me they already took your statement," I said. "Why didn't you say anything?"

"I don't remember anything that happened after I got to the Pub. Honey told me you guys saw the whole thing."

Rhys and I told him what happened. I held up the coin he'd given me. "Do you remember giving me this? You said we were cursed."

He waved it off. "Keep it. I kept it as a good luck charm more than anything. You're on their radar now, same as me and Honey. Watch your back."

"So you know who they are," said Rhys.

"It's a partial list. Of the original Penfield Eight, only Honey is still alive. The cult membership has grown a lot in the past decade. I only care about the ranking members. John and Liddy aren't the only sorcerers anymore. There are business owners and local politicians who've acquired enough power to participate the rituals. Now that I've got some license plate numbers, it'll be easier to identify them. I underestimated them in the past, and that got Nate killed." He winced. "You can see what a good job I've made of it."

"Stop blaming yourself, Lou." Honey patted his

arm. "It was Nate's idea. He could be so bull-headed at times."

"I shouldn't have let Nate talk me into going to that restaurant. It was owned by one of the sorcerers in John's inner circle. Nate was determined to show the Fewkes he wasn't going to back off, and I wasn't about to let him go on his own. We wore our uniforms, so they'd be sure to recognize us." Lou said. "Dumb, dumb, dumb. I'm more careful now. But they're also a lot more dangerous. Jim Reynolds is right to leave them alone--I'd like to keep him and his people out of it."

Lou took a sip of water. "A week after Nate died, the restaurant owner committed suicide. Case closed, even though the gun used in the suicide had been fired twice."

"A cynic would say that wasn't suicide," I suggested.

"Fewkes has a way of making people come around to his point of view."

"So why come after you now? After all this time"

"Whoever it was who saw us that night must've known my car. John Fewkes has been biding his time, I think. Waiting for the right moment." Lou said. "Based on what we saw, they're preparing for a major summoning. They've got the circle laid out and they've layered protections around it. They've stored up far too much power to be anything harmless. Something tells me they've been planning this for a very long time. They'll need a blood offering--maybe even a sacrifice." He looked worn out.

"Samhain, then," said Rhys.

"Yeah. All Hallow's Eve," agreed Lou. That's gotta be it. There's a void moon that night. It's too big a coincidence. I've got to stop that ritual."

"If it's a demon, I can banish it." I said. "Before it has a chance to do anything."

"You gave me your word that you'd stay away from them, Mattie." Lou snapped. "I'm holding you to it."

"Not all demons are the same," Rhys said. "There is no way to tell whether you have enough juice to stop it. Lou is right. The ritual has to be stopped before this thing comes through."

"I'm just trying to help," I said. Besides, you said yourself; I'm already on their radar. I can't just stand on the sidelines. You need me."

"Listen Mattie," Lou said. "John and Liddy have dedicated themselves to the study of the dark arts and the use of sorcery to achieve their goals. Whatever it is they think this creature can give them, you can be assured they'll sacrifice anyone or anything that stands in their way. Once the ritual begins, it will be too late. And you can be sure the site will be protected from outside interference."

"How do you expect to stop them," Honey asked. "You can't have them arrested. Even if you knew the names of everyone in the cult, you can't very well kidnap the whole coven."

I nodded. "She's right. They're not breaking any laws until a demon answers their summons, and by that time, it's too late. We need a plan."

"Stay out of it, Mattie." Lou lay back against his pillow. Dark circles ringed his eyes. He looked exhausted.

Honey stood. "It's late. I need to get home." She had dark circles under her eyes, too. "All this talk has me worried about the boys."

"Be careful," Lou said. "Keep your doors and windows locked. Remember, the Fewkes aren't finished with you yet."

"I think about it every day." She slipped on her coat. "Get some rest."

As soon as she was gone, Lou said. "You've got to get me out to that ritual site, Rhys. I'm the only one that can stop this. I'll be out of here tomorrow morning. If I'm in position a couple hours before midnight, they'll never know I'm there." His eyes fluttered and closed. A moment later, he was sound asleep.

"If their plan was to keep Lou out of the way, they did a good job of it," Rhys said. "He's lucky it wasn't permanent."

"This time," I agreed. "You know he can't do this by himself. I have an idea."

"What do you have in mind," he asked.

"Let's go check out that ritual site in the daylight."

CHAPTER 13

FRIDAY WAS GORGEOUS. Warm temperatures, low humidity, and a soft breeze made the weather feel more like summer than fall. Rhys didn't have classes, and with my hours at work cut back, I was off, too. We rode our bikes out to Knutt's Apple farm, cruising slowly along Plank Road near the orchards until I found a dirt track that looked familiar. We parked the bikes in the shade of the same blue spruce where Lou had parked his Subaru.

Dried cornstalks cackled in the breeze as we walked up the double track. Somehow, the distance seemed further in the daylight, and the lack of cars or any sign of life had me feeling uneasy. Finally, the road curved left, as I remembered, and we caught sight of the barn. In the daylight, the long-abandoned structure was a ramshackle affair. So old, that the roof had partially collapsed—not a trace of paint remained.

I spotted the trail Lou and I had forged through waist-high thistles, and led the way, glad for my leather jacket to fight the thorns. The air grew eerily still, the quiet broken only by the rough call of a crow flying overhead. I couldn't help but feel we were being watched.

We passed the barn, and I paused to get my bearings. The apple orchard stretched before us to the top of a rise about a quarter mile away. Once we reached the trees, the thistles disappeared and we made better progress. I showed Rhys the break where the wire had been cut, and we exited the orchard. The trees and mixed scrub thinned as the land rose beneath our feet.

At the crest of the hill, the old cemetery stretched out before us in a shallow vale—neglected and long forgotten. Most of the headstones had been toppled. Many lay broken. Halfway down the hill, the large tomb I remembered dominated the graveyard. Sheltered beneath a stand of overgrown evergreens, it loomed over the boneyard like sentinel. Instinctively, Rhys and I walked angled our way toward it.

In the deepest shadows, moss and lichen covered the stone walls of the crypt. I shivered in the sudden chill, but there was nothing supernatural about the place. At least, nothing I could sense.

Wordlessly, Rhys pointed out the inscription, scarcely visible through the thick moss:

E M. PENFIELD

1775 - 1794

The epitaph beneath the date was illegible.

"That's an old one," I said. "Maybe even one of the original homesteaders." I made a mental note to have Blix look it up.

We stepped out from the shelter of the memorial, and made our way toward the scraped-out circle at the bottom of the vale.

On closer inspection, there were actually two circles, one within the other. The outer circle circumscribed an area of bare dirt some fifty feet across, surrounding an immense yew tree. The tree appeared to be of great age, with a gnarled and twisted trunk wide enough to drive a car though.

The entire circle, including the area beneath the tree had been cleared of detritus, weeds, and stones, and raked smooth. The smaller, inner summoning circle had been marked off with dark river stones. The inner circle also included the great yew, although it was positioned so that the tree was nearer to one side of the circle. Near the base of the tree, a stone platform had been built up, using several of the old marble headstones stacked on top of each other.

"That altar wasn't there when Lou and I were here before," I said. My voice sounded oddly muffled in the silence. As we drew closer, my feeling of apprehension grew. In the shelter of the vale, the sun felt warmer. I took off my leather jacket and tied it around my waist. "There's something not right about this place."

Rhys scanned the low hills around us with a critical eye. "They picked a good spot. No road access and no neighbors. The only way in or out is on foot. Be tough for anyone to sneak in without being spotted."

Instinctively, I moved toward the tree.

"I wouldn't cross the line of the outer circle," Rhys said. "They've done to an awful lot of preparation here."

"What'll happen if I do?"

He shook his head. "Maybe nothing. But if Lou is right, and the cult has been layering up some sort of power reserve, our sorcerer friends would notice a disruption. It might be warded."

I held Lou's coin at the edge of the dirt circle, at the point where it met with the overgrown grass. Other than the glow it possessed when I held it, the coin did not react. Cautiously. I held out my hand to the invisible plane defining the outer circle. The crescent moon scar on the palm of my hand tingled. I wiped my hand on my jeans. "I think you're right."

I stared up at the tree. Yew was a pretty common tree, but it wasn't native to upstate New York. I'd rarely seen one so big. It must've been planted a long time ago.

"What are you thinking?" asked Rhys.

"Why did they build the summoning circle around the tree? It doesn't make sense. Why not just make the circle smaller?"

"Maybe they're using the tree as the vessel to store their power." Rhys rubbed his jaw. "If Lou were here, he could tell us."

The longer I looked at the setup, the more certain I became that there was something really wrong about that tree.

"Look." I pointed to the large crypt monument. "That tomb looks like it was built to face the tree. It could have been built the same time the tree was planted" I pulled my phone out of my jacket pocket and snapped a few pictures of the circles, the tree, the tomb, and the altar. "Do you think they're planning a human sacrifice?"

"I do. That setup tells me they're playing for keeps."

"If Lou was their intended victim, they'll try again. He's helpless in that cast."

"Lou is tough, Mattie. He's one of the cunning folk."

I frowned. "Honey said the something similar. I don't think it means what I think it does."

"It's a term from Roman times, used by common folk to describe a white wizard."

"He's a witch?" I shook my head. "That can't be. Lou doesn't have a lifeline. He's not human."

"No, not a witch—definitely not human. Lou comes from an ancient line of wizards--like the Merlin. Cunning folk have a single purpose—to root out wielders of malevolent magic and destroy evil. In ancient times, they removed curses and hexes. They are driven to seek out and destroy those who practice the dark arts. It makes perfect sense that he could have become a cop. John and Liddy must suspect what he is. This is a feud that won't end until one of the parties is dead."

"Lou can't walk. He can hardly move. We've got to help him, Rhys." I was getting angrier by the minute. "They've ignored him for years. If they're making their move now, it's got to be something big."

"Tomorrow night is a void moon. We'll need to check the exact time. This ceremony they're planning could very well have been in the works for years. Come on, I've seen enough here." Rhys and I retraced our steps back to where we'd parked the bikes.

Overhead, a mob of angry crows attacked and harried a lone hawk out of their territory--the raucus sounds of their cawing must've carried for miles.

"We only need to disrupt their focus long enough so that the summoning loses momentum and the power dissipates. Let it build, and then cut it off mid-stream. They won't have time to rebuild the power layers and use them the same night. They'll have to start over. That will give is more time."

"If we could get our hands on some dynamite, we could just blow this place up," I said. I was only half-kidding. "That'll stop them."

"There's my warrior princess." He pulled me close and kissed my forehead. "No explosives."

"Flaming arrows, then. We could shoot them right at the tree. That should do it."

He laughed. "Possibly. Reynolds already thinks you're a fire bug, it might bring the cavalry down on us."

"Hey, the Sheriff likes me." But Rhys was right. My mind raced. "I've got an idea."

"Tell me."

"I've got to talk to someone, first. I'll tell you as

soon as I can."

"Still don't trust me, eh?"

I grabbed him by his shirt, pulled him close and kissed him. It was a good kiss, long and deep. "I trust you with my life, Rhys, and that's the truth."

And then I told him about the dreamspider, Luçien Bold.

All of it. From the first dream of guilty pleasure to the deepest shame I'd ever experienced, and my unrepentant joy at seeing his bones picked clean by Dave's piranhas.

"I hated myself. I felt dirty and stupid. I'd invited him into my dreams, and it was my fault I couldn't make him stop. I thought if you knew what I was really like, you'd be disgusted with me, just like I was, and that you'd think I'd wanted it to happen. But you never said a word; you never pushed me, even though I knew you wanted me."

I found a rumpled tissue in my jacket pocket and blew my nose. "I felt so ugly. I couldn't stand to look at myself in the mirror. I couldn't stand to be touched. But after a while, you convinced me that your feelings for me were real. And that in your eyes, I was something special. And you were so frikking great and I didn't deserve it. I didn't deserve you."

He wiped a tear off my cheek with his thumb.

"I wasn't going to tell you, Rhys. Not ever. I didn't want it to change things between us. I guess what I'm trying to say is that I really do. Trust you."

And then it was as if the dam broke and all the words came rushing out. "And I wish I were immortal, but I'm not and I'm terrified you'll leave and even more scared that you'll stay with me until I'm old and ugly out of some sort of warped loyalty. And it won't be right because even if you loved me enough to stay, it's not natural and--."

He pulled me into a big bear hug.

He spoke softly, into my hair, his words for my ears alone. "You talk in your sleep, sweet thing. I figured it out that first night. You relived it every night in your dreams. It didn't say anything because I didn't want to make your pain any worse. It wasn't your fault. You didn't do anything wrong. They needed to die."

I melted into him, his words a balm for my soul. "Thank you for saying that." My lips trembled.

"I hoped you'd tell me someday. That you did today means more than I can say. Nothing will ever change the way I feel about you."

Feeling at peace for the first time in a very long time, I nodded mutely.

"Like you said, I'm immortal. We're different. I can't change what I am. Whatever you decide, for however long you'll have me, I am yours, Mattie. You said you trust me with your life, and that means the world to me. I want you to know that I trust you with my death."

CHAPTER 14

IT WAS DUSK when Rhys and I got home. We parked the bikes out front, and walked up to the porch together. A cloud of will-o-the-wisps appeared from nowhere. As they had the previous times, the tiny lights swarmed and pelted us like manic confetti.

Rhys and I just stood there, grinning like a couple idiots, our hands held out in wonder as they danced around us. It was like a fairyland.

"They're at it again," Rhys's expression was like a kid at his first carnival. "What are they saying?"

Loosa-loosa-loo. Loosa-loosa-loose.

"Same as before," I said. "Can't you hear them? They're all saying it at the same time, so it kind of echoes."

As sudden as they appeared, the lights zoomed up

and away. Like campfire sparks into the night sky.

So cool. "This is the third time. It's got to mean something. I keep meaning to ask Charlie about them."

We went inside, still a little dazed. I slipped out of my leather jacket and hung it on the coat rack in the entry hall. "Honey told me the Senequois believe that will-o-the-wisps are some sort of mystic spirit messengers."

"I didn't realize you and Honey were such good buddies."

"I like her," I admitted. "She's been a lot friendlier since I started working with Lou."

I told him about Honey being one of the original Penfield witches and that the Fewkes had been stalking and intimidating her since Nate's death.

He gave a low whistle. "It really puts Lou's so-called accident in a whole new light, doesn't' it?"

"Yeah, it does. Except for Honey, none of the Penfield Eight are still alive. I don't think she has many woman friends." Neither did I, come to think of it. I didn't hang out with the other parking control officers anymore. Heck, I hadn't been asked to join the department's fall bowling league this year, either. I couldn't remember the last time I'd stopped in at the Stick and Stein for beer after work. Honey had been out of the coven for years. We had more in common than I'd originally thought.

"If those women we saw in Growlers are representative of the cult, I can see why."

Something clicked into place. "Growlers Pub is less than a mile from that old farmhouse house Charlie and I cleared. The realtor told me it had been a foreclosure. Vacant for years. What if it belonged to the Fewkes?"

"Easy enough to check," said Rhys.

"I banished a named djemon from that house. It was playing poltergeist with the light bulbs, slamming cupboards, and generally scaring off buyers. Maybe it wasn't just for spite. What if the previous owners knew about the trapped spirits?" The more I thought about it, the more it made sense to me. "What if the house and the Penfield witch cult and the summoning ritual are all connected? What if the will-o-the-wisps we saw tonight really are spirit messengers, trying to warn us?"

"You want to talk to Charlie."

"I think it's about time, don't you?" I reached for my jacket.

"I like the way you think, lady."

141

We found Charlie at home in his brown and white cabin in the Shore Happy Motor Court, a dismal collection of one-room cottages built decades ago as seasonal employee housing for the amusement park. Most of the buildings had decayed to a somewhat less than seedy state—Charlie's being a notable exception. A layer of white quartz gravel kept the weeds at bay in the front garden. Black wrought iron trimmed the solid oak front door, and red and white striped curtains graced the windows. Red plastic flowers in the window boxes gave the cottage a dignified look that made the other cabins seem drearier by comparison.

Inside, a colorful orange, red, and yellow wool rug covered polished wood floors with a primitive geometric pattern. The main living and seating area consisted of a worn brown recliner and small sofa. Beneath the front window, a fake fireplace warmed the room with cheery simulated flames. On one wall, a cabinet disguised the pull-down Murphy bed. Opposite the window, a built-in banquette, sink, two-burner hotplate and countertop refrigerator made up his kitchen and dining area.

Annie lay curled up in her sheepskin-lined doggie bed next to Charlie's recliner, her gaze fixed on her master. I asked Charlie about the will-o-the-wisps. "When it happened to us that first time, you said it was a warning."

"An omen, if you like." Charlie answered, nodding.

"Honey Briscoe told me that the Senequois people believe that these lights are spirit messengers. She told me that the message can only be heard by the person who is meant to receive it."

When he wasn't wearing his security guard uniform, it was much easier to believe that Charlie was a shaman of the Senequois people. Dressed simply, in a faded pair of old jeans, a button-front red flannel shirt with the sleeves rolled up to his elbows, and an old pair of scuffed moccasins, his voice and bearing proclaimed him still very much a man of his people.

"Do you think the swamp lights we saw that night were the trapped spirits you released from the house?"

"I don't believe so. Trapped souls ain't the same as spirit messengers. The People believe they can travel between the worlds of the living and the dead. Will-o-the-wisps tain't neither nor."

I sagged against the back of the couch. "So you don't think that the message I got tonight came from the trapped souls you released."

Charlie gave me a puzzled look. "I asked you if you could feel them spirits when we walked into the house that day. You said no."

"I couldn't. But when the will-o-the-wisps attacked

us on the porch, they spoke to me. It's happened three times, now, and they said the same thing every time."

He leaned forward, his elbows on his knees, frowning. "Jaysus Mary of Morgantown. You say you heard 'em speak?"

"Yeah. They said loosa loosa, or something like that. I just assumed you'd heard it too."

"I didn't hear it, but I believe she heard something." Rhys said.

"Honey thought they might be speaking the language of the Senequois people. That's why we came over here. Does it mean anything to you?"

"Gimme a minute." Charlie got up and walked to one of the cupboards in his kitchen and took down a quart-sized canning jar, half-filled with a dark liquid. He unscrewed the lid and the liquid became a smoky mist. It drifted up from within the jar. Charlie closed his eyes, inhaled a lungful of the vapor, then resealed the jar and replaced it in the cabinet. He stood motionless, his eyes closed, his palms held up as if in supplication for a long moment, and gradually exhaled, nodding slightly.

Annie gave a soft chirrup as he returned to his chair. His eyes had an unfocused look.

Rhys and I exchanged a look. This couldn't be good.

Charlie wiped his mouth and began to speak. His

voice sounded faint at first, as if recalling some faraway memory, but gradually grew stronger.

"In the beginning, there was the land. And from the land, the creator fashioned the first People. And the People crawled from the land and lived in the light. And they hunted and gathered food from the bounty of the land, and they raised their children to do the same.

"But there was one who did not like the light. He did not want to live among the People. He was a shape-changer. Sometimes, he took the shape of a night-raven. At other times he was a long narrow man with pointed ears, and glowing red eyes who crawled along his stomach like a snake.

"And it was said that when people allowed dark or depressing thoughts to enter their minds, it crept inside them and consumed their essence, leaving only a ravenous, hungry husk behind. And it was also said that disobedient children were lured into the forest, where it took them for its own. It could bewitch hunters by mimicking the cry of a wounded animal, and when they followed the sound into the woods, it would prick them with a thorn that would enslave them to its terrible bidding. As its strength and appetites grew, stories were told of unhappily married women stolen from their homes by the tall, narrow man, never to be seen again. When the first swamp lights appeared, it was said they were the children of this spirit and the stolen women of the People.

"The People named this creature *Nalusa Falaya*, and it was an immortal evil of great and terrible power.

"And it is said among the People that the Nalusa Falaya claimed the great forests where the Senequois people lived and the banks of the Great Spirit Lake as his own. And it saw the how the water sparkled and the People lived in peace and harmony with the land and it despised such order and harmony. It demanded human sacrifice, and when the People refused it swore to eat the souls of everyone in the tribe. For many years, the tribe was preyed upon by the evil being. By the time the first white settlers arrived, the great Senequois nation had been reduced to a single clan. Eventually the shaman of the clan trapped the spirit, and imprisoned the Nalusa Falaya in a spirit tree, where it remains to this day."

Charlie shook his head. "I can think of no other meaning for the warning of the swamp lights. That 'loosa loose' you heard sounds to me like someone is plannin' to release the Nalusa Falaya."

Rhys and I exchanged a silent look.

Charlie pressed his lips together. "I don't think it's possible. It makes no sense why anyone would. It's a powerful, evil thing."

"I've witnessed the containment of a powerful demon only once," Rhys said. "This was in Europe. The trap required a heavy buildup of concentrated power wrapped around an enticing lure. The king's sorcerer sacrificed the lives of a dozen prisoners to bait the trap. Once the summoned deity had materialized inside the circle, the power crucible held it secure until it was forced into a prepared containment vessel and sealed."

Jeeze. "What kind of vessel?"

"It depends on how dangerous the entity is, and how long it must be imprisoned. In the case of djenie, it could be something as portable and innocuous as a lamp." Rhys said, with a look of distaste. "For the Merlin, only a crystal-lined cave would work."

"No," Charlie said. "There was no cave. An' no box could contain the Nalusa Falaya. The People trapped the evil creature in a spirit tree. In this instance, every part of the tree is poisonous—the poison saturates the spirit and keeps the creature weak--unable to take shape and escape."

"Where is this spirit tree?" asked Rhys.

"It has to be that big yew tree," I said. "Inside the old cemetery. I got a really bad feeling from that tree."

"That makes sense," Rhys agreed. "I felt the same way."

I pulled the coin Lou had given me from my pocket

and showed it to Charlie. "Lou says this can detect black magic. I'll bet that if I touched it to the bark of that tree, we'd know for sure."

The People believe that any spirit held inside a spirit tree takes on the characteristics of the spirit tree. The tree holding the Nalusa Falaya captive is especially accursed."

"If we cross that circle, I'm convinced the cult will know," Rhys said.

"Yeah, but if we chop it down before the ritual, that'll kill it. The summoning won't work, right Charlie?"

The old man frowned. "The spirit is immortal. Cuttin' down a spirit tree won't destroy the spirit trapped inside. Nor will burnin' it. It will only kill the tree. Over time, the spirit would eventually gather itself together and escape. No one in their right mind would do such a thing."

"That explains the double circle," I said. "The Fewkes must want something from it."

"No," Charlie said. "The Nalusa Falaya is an ancient creature. It has nothing to offer but death."

"Based on what we've heard, I doubt that concerns the Fewkes." Rhys said. "If this demon could grant them immortality, or power, or wealth, or knowledge, or anything else they believe they must have, chances are the Fewkes plan to negotiate for what they want in exchange for giving it its freedom."

"That's crazy," I said. "Surely they're not going to actually set it free."

Rhys made a face. "I expect they're confident they can get it back in the tree once it's given them what they want. Although they'd need the same kind of bait to release it that they used to trap it." Rhys said. "We're talking about couple dozen victims here."

The answer hit me like a punch in the chest. "Charlie, you said it was a soul eater. Couldn't they use trapped souls?" I could hardly get the words out. "Like the ones trapped in that house. Maybe they were just being stored in the house until they were needed. That's gotta be it—Charlie, you said they were scared. Terrified. At the time, I didn't believe you. I mean, what do the dead have to be afraid of? But being consumed by the Nalusa Falaya, that would scare them, wouldn't it?"

Charlie looked positively ill. "Mebbe. It was Senequois magic used to trap the Nalusa Falaya. One of the People would have to be present during the ceremony. Not many left."

"What about one of the cult members?" I asked.

Charlie gave a snort. "Ain't a single drop of Senequois blood in any of 'em anymore."

"Honey and her grandmother are both Senequois. And both of them were members of the Penfield eight."

"Not many know that," admitted Charlie.

"She also said that her Grandmother died shortly after she moved in with the Fewkes. She was a full-blooded Senequois. Her spirit could have been trapped in that house for years."

"Good night," Rhys said.

"That would do it," Charlie agreed. "I heard them souls screamin' from the banister as soon as I walked in. Makes me double glad I released 'em."

A shiver crept up my spine. Something he said tickled a memory, but then it was gone.

"If they plan to put the Nalusa Falaya back in the spirit tree, they're gonna need a whole lot more souls than they planned to replace all them ones we freed," Charlie said.

Shit. "Thanks, Charlie. We gotta go," I said. Rhys was already moving toward the door.

"Where you goin'?"

"Halloween is tomorrow," I said. "Gotta see a man about a wolf."

CHAPTER 15

RHYS AND I arrived home in the pre-dawn hours of Saturday morning, intent on grabbing a few hours of sleep. Rhys stumbled upstairs to bed, while I put Blix to work on the Internet.

Three hours later, we were up. We had a lot to do today, and not much time to get it done. Rhys had already left.

Blix had not been able to find any information on the Internet on how to stop a demon summoning. I guess everyone wants to learn how to summon one, not how to screw one up. And while there was a lot of information online about many different kinds of demons and evil spirits, he'd found next to nothing on the Nalusa Falaya.

Blix still couldn't speak yet, but his wings had completely sprouted from his shoulders over the past few days; ever since he'd started reading and researching for me. He couldn't actually fly, but that didn't stop him from jumping across the room and flapping them at every opportunity. His inability to speak didn't prevent him from communicating any more. He was so good with my cell phone keypad, I'd gotten him his own phone so he could text me.

Maybe you are over thinking this, he texted. *Perhaps there is no special way to break up a summoning, other than causing a distraction. Simply crossing the plane of the summoning circle could do it.*

"I hope you're right, Blix. Keep digging, and text me if you find anything. I'll be back in a few hours."

Doc had called to let me know that my car was ready. As much as I loved the bike, the streak of summer temperatures we'd been enjoying was at an end. Forecasters were predicting snow within the next few days. As much as I loved riding the Vic, I was looking forward to using the Honda's heater.

Lou was being released from the hospital this afternoon. I'd promised Honey I'd drop by with a load of groceries and help her set up the hospital bed at his place.

I turned over the Vic to Doc and paid him what I owed, then drove out to Henrietta to the

Outdoorsman's Cavern to pick up a few essentials we'd need tonight. Given that hunting season was in full swing, the place was packed, but I managed to score a lightweight cot we could use as a stretcher for carrying Lou, flashlights, batteries, and even a couple air horns that were on sale. After a drive over to Wegmans in Pittsford for groceries, I was feeling pretty confident that our plan was going to work.

I just had one more stop to make.

The Shore Haven Public Library was located on 6th Street, between Empress and St. Leonard. Built in the 1940s, the squat, two-story building had been renovated several times over the years, but to me, it still looked the same as it had when I was a kid. Built of rough-hewn grey granite, it resembled a prison more than a temple of learning. Only the stone courtyard in front, rimmed with bright orange marigolds and benches, softened the severity of the place. A wide stairway led up to the double doors, and once inside, the narrow windows and deep sills made for a perpetually gloomy interior.

I entered the vestibule, where dozens of jackets in a variety of colors and sizes hung from wall hooks placed at varying heights around the room, awaiting the return of their owners. It looked like Saturday was busy day. In a month, down parkas would line the walls and the place would look like a patchwork padded cell.

I stepped up to the information desk, where an older woman appraised me with a bored expression. My friend Karen used to work here, but she left six months ago, and this woman didn't look familiar. Silver hair cut shorter than mine and cat's eye glasses gave her a decidedly un-librarian-like look. Kind of arty. Maybe she was a volunteer.

"Can I help you find a book?" She asked.

"Um, I'm looking for the demon section."

She gave me a disapproving look. "Excuse me?"

"Or sorcery. Specifically. I'm looking for any information you might have on summoning a demon."

She picked up a pencil twiddled it between her thumb and forefinger. "What is the name of the book?"

Yeah, I really hadn't thought this through. "I don't know the name of the book."

"The author then."

"Can't you just point me to the demon section?"

She gave me an angry, doubtful look that I remembered from every teacher I ever had in Junior High. "Wait right here." She marched swiftly to the far side of the library and spoke to a dark-haired, younger woman replacing books on the shelves from a cart. The two women spoke for several minutes, all the while, glancing sharply over at me.

I was just about to slink out, when the second of the two women approached. The crescent-shaped scar on the palm of my hand began to itch like crazy. A rush of adrenaline spiked through me. The woman was no djemon. And she had a lifeline, which ruled out a vampire or any other sort of undead. She was human, but something about the way she looked at me reminded me of the women at Growlers. My heart skipped a beat.

Could she be one of the cultists? A sorceress?

Oh jeeze. Maybe this wasn't such a good idea. I really should have talked to Lou first.

My hand began to burn, warning me to get out. I backed away. "Um, never mind." I said.

She stopped just short of the information desk, watching me, not saying a word. She was about my height and wore her long brown hair pulled back in a single braid. She wore a simple black t-shirt and skirt which accentuated her wiry, muscular build. She didn't look like a librarian, either.

I edged my way toward the vestibule, but with each step, my feet and legs became heavier—as if I were wading through invisible quicksand. I didn't know what was going on, but whatever it was, I trusted the little voice in my head, telling me to *get the frack out of here!* My heart pounded.

As hard as I tried, I could not take another step.

The dark-haired librarian raised an eyebrow at my predicament, a look of sly amusement on her face.

Morta's shears slid into my hand and reflexively. I clenched and released my fist. The scissor action seemed to diminish the sluggishness in my leaden legs.

She closed the distance between us, stopping just out of arm's reach.

I held up my shears. No one else in the library seemed to see me, or notice anything at all.

"You don't belong here," the librarian said. "We don't serve your kind." The weight around my legs seemed to increase. I flexed the shears again.

"It's a public place," I said. "I don't like bullies." As a kid from the wrong side of the tracks, I'd met more than my share of them. I probably had ten pounds on her, but she was solid muscle.

She gave me a superior sort of sneer. "Maybe I'll just hold you there and call the Sheriff."

I know a bluff when I see one. She wasn't going to call anybody. Two could play that game. I pulled my newly organized cell phone out of my pocket. "Yes, by all means, let's call Sheriff Jim. He's a good friend of mine." Well, maybe I was stretching it a little. "Better yet, I've got the FBI on speed dial."

The heaviness around my legs lifted so suddenly, I

fell right on my ass. Of course, everyone in the library saw that. I scrambled to my feet, and got out of there, the sound of the women's mocking laughter ringing in my ears.

Lou and Honey lived on St. Drogo's Street. Most of the streets in Shore Haven are named after obscure Saints or Tarot Cards. Every school-aged kid in Shore Haven knew that Saint Drogo had been a shepherd in 12th century France who possessed the magical ability to be in two places at once. He was the patron saint of deformities, mental illness, and coffee houses.

I arrived at the duplex where Honey and Lou lived around three o'clock--later than planned, but it couldn't be helped. Unlike many of the wood-shingle beach cottages in the neighborhood, the duplex was yellow Tudor-style stucco with a steeply-pitched roof and dark brown trim. Each side of the duplex had its own entry and tiny walled garden in the front. On Lou's side, the garden consisted of a fountain and patio with potted plants, now withered and brown, while on the opposite side, an unraked lawn and paved walkway were strewn with plastic toy soldiers and a soccer ball with practice net.

Lou's door was wide open when I arrived, and the hospital bed had already been delivered, and was sitting in the middle of the front room. Nine year-old Arby was seated at Lou's dining room table, drawing a 'welcome home' picture on poster paper.

"Oh good," Honey checked her watch and flashed a harried smile. "Nate Junior is at a friend's, so you can help me with the bed. Knowing Lou, I doubt he'll be needing it for very long."

She turned to her son. "Pick up those crayons and go on home. You've got homework to finish. Mattie can help me with the rest of this."

"Okay, Mama." Arby slipped from the table and carefully set his drawing on the adjustable bed table that had been delivered with the hospital bed. He gave me a thoughtful look.

Arby was a typical kid, with grass stains on the knees of his jeans, his shirttail hanging out. In looks and his stocky build, he took after his father more than Honey, although he shared her Senequois features and coloring. His eyes were so dark, they appeared almost black—he actually reminded me a little of Charlie. Old man's eyes.

"Hi Arby, remember me? I'm Mina's aunt Mattie."

"He shook his head. "No. That's not right." He pointed at my poison-blackened hand. "You're the dead hand lady."

"Um." I glanced at Honey, uncertain.

"Good heavens. Out of the mouths of babes," Honey murmured, as she rushed him out the door. "Off you go. No TV until your homework is done, right?"

"Sorry, Mattie." She grabbed a folded bed sheet and shook it out.

I reached for the other side, and we smoothed the fabric across the mattress. "What was that all about?"

"He's got the sight," she said. "He takes after my grandmother. Three hundred years ago, he would have been apprenticed to the tribal shaman. But now," she gave me a wistful expression and tucked a corner of the sheet beneath the mattress. "There isn't anyone to teach him the old ways. He sees so much he doesn't understand yet. When he looks at you, I imagine he sees your affinity for spirits and demons. He means no offense; he just doesn't have the vocabulary."

"Don't worry about it. I've been called a lot worse."

I explained what Charlie had told us about the swamp lights and the Nalusa Falaya. "Lou and Charlie both think that the cult is going to try to summon it tonight. We have a plan to disrupt the ritual and stop them."

"I've never liked Halloween. I'm keeping the boys inside with me tonight." She stood at the big picture window and looked up and down the street. "Where is he? The Medi-Van should have arrived hours ago." The cast on Lou's leg made it impossible for him to get into a car. "I'm going to call the hospital and see what's taking so long. You want some coffee? I can make a fresh pot."

"Coffee sounds good," I said. "He's checking out against doctors orders. Maybe there's a problem with the paperwork. I'll finish up here and be right over."

She gave me a little wave and left. I shook out two cotton blankets and smoothed them over the top sheet, recognizing the familiar scent of Stay Fresh dryer sheets. Same brand I used. I folded the down comforter Honey had retrieved from Lou's upstairs bedroom and placed it at the foot of the bed. Although the hospital bed dominated the room, the rest of Lou's place was modest and neat. Clearly, he'd been a bachelor a long time, and was good at it. A better housekeeper than me, come to think of it. I washed and dried the few dishes in the sink, put away the groceries, and plumped up the bed pillows before giving the place a final inspection. A pair of framed photos flanked the fireplace mantel–an old one of Lou and his partner Nate in uniform, and a more recent one of Lou standing companionably between Nate Junior and Arby. All three of them were holding fishing poles and laughing.

Nice.

CHAPTER 16

TEN MINUTES LATER, I walked over to Honey's side of the duplex. I knocked on the door, but there was no answer. It wasn't locked, so I let myself in. Unsurprisingly, the inside layout was a mirror image of Lou's place. "Hello?"

The house echoed, as if no one was home.

Something's not right here. I made my way to the kitchen, and froze. An open can of Folgers coffee lay to the floor; dark grounds had spilled across the linoleum. Even an apprentice private detective like me could see at least four sets of shoeprints in the grounds. A scuffle. The back door was wide open.

I stepped around the coffee and out the back door. The lawn had been recently raked, and the patio table and chairs neatly covered in canvas for the winter. A gate leading to the alley behind the house was ajar.

The alley was empty.

"Honey?" I ran back to the house in a panic. "Arby!"

I checked every room, but the place was empty. In the kid's room, on the floor between the twin beds, I found a crudely carved snake-like figure sitting on a blood-smeared page of lined notepaper. A message had been cut from newspaper headlines and glued to the note:

The day of reckoning has finally arrived.
You know where to find us.

The carved fetish began to emit an unnatural mist. Like a fog, it surrounded me—cold as ice. I backed out of the room, my heart racing. Holy shit. Lou had been right all along. *Lou.*

I dialed the hospital and asked for Lou Scali.

"He's been released," the nurse said.

"How long ago?" I asked, my throat dry.

"They left mid-morning." She sounded harried.

"Has the driver come back yet?"

She made an exasperated sound. "No he hasn't and I've got three people here waiting on him. Lenny usually calls if he's going to be late. He's not answering his phone."

I hung up. The hospital was ten minutes away. No reason it should take so long. This was bad news.

The consequences of Charlie releasing the trapped spirits from the Fewkes farmhouse became clear to me.

The Fewkes needed souls to summon the demon. They'd have to replace the souls Charlie freed, and they didn't have much time. That was why Lou, Honey, and Arby had been taken, and there were probably other victims as well. Thank goodness Nate Junior hadn't been home. I hoped he was safe.

How many souls had the Fewkes planned to use to summon the Nalusa Falaya? I didn't want to think about it.

Dark had come early this Halloween.

If I called 911, they wouldn't consider it an emergency. The victims had only been gone a couple hours. I called Sheriff Reynolds' cell phone instead. He answered straight away. "I'm kind of busy here Mattie."

I could hear sirens in the background. It wasn't even full dark yet. All the crazies come out on Halloween.

"I'm at Lou Scali's place. He was checked out of the hospital in a med-van before noon, but it never arrived. The driver is also missing, and he's not answering his phone."

"It's going to have to wait. I've got shots fired at the Halloween Event in Mumford. Everybody's in costume and the power is out. It's darker than Hades out here. Can't tell what's going on."

Mumford was twenty miles away. The Historic Village was a living museum of impeccably preserved 19th century buildings set out in the middle of nowhere. Their traditional Halloween event attracts hundreds of kids and families every year.

"Honey Briscoe and her son Arby are missing, too. I think they've been kidnapped. There's a bloody note here. Something's going down tonight, I know it."

"Shit." Reynolds said. I heard screams in the background. I didn't know if he was cursing at me or them. "Stay right there. I'll send somebody when I can."

"I can't wait—." He'd already hung up.

I paced the hall between Honey's kitchen and Arby's bedroom, my gut twisting tighter with every step. They might already be dead. Or would the Fewkes keep them alive and sacrifice them on the altar?

Guilt tore at me. I'd thought we'd have more time. I really never imagined they'd come after Honey. And after ten years? This was insane.

The timetable had been moved up and we weren't ready. We'd hadn't planned on getting to the ritual site for at least another couple of hours. I called Rhys and told him what had happened. "The Sheriff has his hands full right now; we're on our own, Rhys."

"I'll call Kevin and tell him," he said. "I need to make a stop at Charlie's, and then I'll pick you up."

"Charlie's? What for? We agreed to keep him out of this."

"We're not going in there unarmed. We need weapons."

"Guns won't stop a demon." I'd argued with him earlier, about the need for weapons at all. All we needed to do was to disrupt the ceremony. Whatever the cultists were dabbling in, they were human, and therefore protected by law. But that was before. Things had gone nasty in a hurry.

"I'm not talking about guns. Charlie has the key to the fun house."

When Rhys had gone back to Scotland to close up his personal affairs, he'd run into a bit of trouble. A few of the druids took exception to his plans to leave the Order. When they tried to stop him, he escaped through the underworld, where they couldn't follow. It was why he couldn't call me when he was gone. He had stored some of his weapons and more precious possessions beneath the Fun House portal, where no mortal could reach them.

"You waited until now to get them?"

"The plan can still work, only the timeline has moved. Wait for me." The stress in his voice made me realize how worried he really was.

"No can do, Rhys. I'll meet you there." I hung up and ran to my car. No point in arguing. It would take me almost an hour to get to the cemetery and hike in.

I hoped I wasn't too late.

CHAPTER 17

A BARRICADE HAD been set up across the dirt track access road. Two guys stood guard. Not obviously armed, but I doubted I'd be able to get past them. I drove by without slowing, and a half-mile later, made a right-hand turn into the parking lot at Knutt's Apple farm. The cider barn and farm market were already closed up for the night. A few pickup trucks were parked in the shadowy darkness at the far end of the lot.

A good sign. It looked like at least some of the werewolves had gotten the word. I parked my car next to them and set off through the dark trees, angling back toward where I knew the barbed-wire fence marked the back of the property line.

"Blix," I said, keeping my voice low. "I summon you."

My little djemon materialized on my left shoulder, and wrapped his tail around my neck for balance, his luminous eyes softly aglow. Djemons see perfectly well, even on the darkest nights. No moon tonight, but the sky was clear, and with the apple trees bare of leaves, the stars provided just enough light to see. Low areas in the orchard held the beginnings of ground fog, giving the scene an eerie feel. Earlier rains had softened the now-decaying carpet of leaves beneath my feet, muffling my footsteps.

"Let me know if you see anybody, Blix."

He nodded, his cheek next to mine. Blix wasn't big or powerful enough to be much use if anyone came after me, but his superior senses would detect anyone hiding close by.

Somewhere up ahead was the crypt where I was supposed to meet up with Kevin, the bartender from Growlers, and an alpha for one of the local werewolf packs.

After what seemed like a very long hike, I reached the fence line marking the back of the apple farm. I had a moment of panic when I remembered that Rhys had the wire cutters, but Blix raced ahead of me and found the spot where the wolves had gone through. He led me straight to the gap beside a mounded pile of clothes and boots hidden beneath a leaf-strewn tarp.

I stepped through gap and climbed up the steep hill which surrounded the cemetery. The still air carried no sound of chanting, as it had when Lou and I had been here previously. I took that as another good sign. They hadn't started yet. Maybe Lou and Honey and Arby were still alive.

The crescent moon on the palm of my hand began to itch and glow.

Yeah, right.

I crested the hill behind a clump of shrubbery. I paused to catch my breath, using Master Foo's breathing techniques. Cautiously, I peered over the bushes to get my bearings.

Oh man. The valley was completely filled with low fog which obliterated the cemetery. I couldn't see a thing. Not even the vault where I was supposed to meet Kevin. From where I was, nothing looked familiar. I didn't dare turn on the flashlight.

A cold nose touched my hand. I jumped, even as I'd half-expected it. Kevin had told me werewolves did not suffer from hunting lust on nights without a full moon, and therefore not as dangerous. I wasn't so sure. The pale monster standing at my hip made me nervous. Bigger than any dog I'd ever seen. Its eyes reflected the pinpoints of starlight with a chilling amber glow.

It gave me a look that clearly said, follow me, and moved toward the fog.

I grabbed onto the shaggy fur at his neck and let him lead me, like a frikking blind woman, into the murk. The mist enveloped us with a clammy, greasy feel—definitely not natural. The stars disappeared—I couldn't see any further than the wolf's ears as he led me down the hill. When I slipped on the wet grass, he braced himself, and I leaned against him for support. The path he chose wove unerringly between the crumbled and toppled headstones.

By the time we neared the meet-up behind the crypt, the mist had thinned enough to see the ritual site. Within the circle itself, a ring of Tiki torches smoked and flickered, illuminating the scene. Thirteen hooded figures were positioned along the outline of a large pentagram. Only the faintest murmur of sound could be heard. I unfocused my vision, and cracked open the little door to Morta's power inside my head. A vague, shimmery image surrounded the summoning circle. The chill of the vault cut through my leather jacket and I shivered—not wholly from the cold. There was no mistaking the scene below—it was the real deal. The ritual had already begun.

Three hooded figures patrolled the outside of the

circle, carrying stun batons. They faced outward from the circle, toward the path that Lou and I had followed that first night. They were expecting trouble. The stun batons would incapacitate anyone who came within reach.

Kevin, wearing only a down parka and a pair of baggy sweatpants, pulled me into the deepest shadows of the vault. The earthy scent of pine and damp earth was strangely comforting. He introduced the white wolf as Silas, an alpha from outside the county who owed him a favor. "Where's Rhys?" He asked.

"He'll be here."

"I don't like this one bit," he said. "You guys didn't say anything about a kid."

Kevin wasn't kidding. There were now three altars lined up at the foot of the spirit tree where there had only been one before.

It broke my heart to see the three of them lined up on separate altars. Honey and Arby lay motionless. I prayed they weren't dead. On the third altar, Lou was awake—trying unsuccessfully to rub his gag loose. All three had their hands bound with zip ties behind their backs. There was a deep-looking cut on Lou's forehead, and his face was covered with dried blood; his body and cast were covered in mud. It looked like they'd dragged him to the altar from the car.

Arby lay on the center altar, his inert form surrounded by twelve wooden figures of varying sizes and complexity. Some were no bigger than my fist—crudely carved dowels with faces drawn on. Others looked like valuable antiques. I recognized the doll which had fallen from Liddy Fewkes's bag and begged for Morta's help. Twelve trapped souls and three live sacrifices. We'd been wrong in assuming the cult would need to obtain more souls to conduct the ritual—they must've been stockpiling them.

Silas perked his ears and chuffed.

"I'm here," Rhys said. "How many wolves do we have?"

My heart skipped a beat at the sight of him. He'd traded in his usual leathers for some sort of scaled body armor—a kilt and breastplate with heavy leather braces and greaves. Rhys carried his great sword, which I had only seen once before, in a sheath strapped across his back, and a shorter sword belted at his waist.

"Five, including me and Silas," answered Kevin.

"Here." Rhys handed me a stiletto as long as my arm. "It's the lightest blade I've got. It's a Kinjali dagger, blessed by Morta herself."

I hefted the weapon. This was no bamboo pole. Longer than my forearm, it felt surprisingly comfortable in my hand. The blade looked razor sharp.

"You keep it," I gave it back to him. "I'd probably stab myself with that thing." I slid the cool shears of the Hand of Fate into my hand and held them up to show him. "I'm better off with these."

"If you want to stop this, we can't wait much longer," Kevin said.

As one, all thirteen of the hooded figures pulled back their hoods, revealing themselves.

John Fewkes, the black sorcerer, stood at the center altar, while at his shoulder, his sister, Liddy, stood at the ready, holding three gleaming knives on a black tray. At a signal from Fewkes, the largest of the cultists approached Liddy and picked up a knife from the tray. He was built like a weight lifter, and completely bald— his scalp tattooed with strange, rune-like symbols. I did not recognize him. He moved to stand at the furthest altar, where Honey lay unconscious.

John took another of the knives from Liddy and held his arms above his head in apparent supplication, over the inert form of Arby, while Liddy took the third knife and took her place at the altar where Lou lay squirming. Although the buildup of power was palpable, we could not hear more than a murmur through the protective circle. The ten-inch blades gleamed in the torchlight like an evil promise.

Inside the circle, a flurry of swamp lights appeared

from out of nowhere. They swarmed the tree, like maddened bees. Whatever doubts I'd had before, I knew Charlie had been right. Unless we stopped them, they intended to sacrifice Lou, Honey, and Arby to the Nalusa Falaya.

"Guys," I said. "Now is the time. Now would be good."

Kevin shook his head. "They won't be able to hear us. The deal is off."

In the eyes of the law, a lycanthrope's actions and movements are strictly regulated, and killing a were in wolf form carries a lesser penalty than killing a real wolf. Any werewolf who threatens, attacks, or willingly transmits the virus to a human being is subject to immediate execution with extreme prejudice; no trial necessary. The only way Rhys and I had been able to convince Kevin and his friends to help us was by assuring them that all they had to do was to howl and show themselves at a distance—harass the coven just enough to distract them and disrupt the ritual.

"Come on, it could still work," I said. "You can't just let them kill three innocent people in cold blood." I could hardly keep still for the need to act. My toes tapped a restless beat to drums only I could hear.

The problem was that the layers of power built up to keep the demon inside the circle worked both ways. They couldn't hear us, so our plan to distract them with noise would not work. It would have to be something already inside the circle. My mind raced, seeking a solution.

Should have brought the flaming arrows, I mused. Louder and louder, the drums in my head sang while Rhys and Kevin argued.

Blix could materialize inside the circle, but what could he do? He didn't have the size or strength to stop this show.

It would take something like Morta's power to disrupt that summoning, and the only way to do it was from inside that circle. I let the drums fill me and flung open the door in my head. Morta's golden light poured through me like adrenaline. *Come on, come on.*

"I can't stand this. I've got to get closer," I said. "There's got to be a way in." Kevin and Rhys both eyed me warily. I pointed to the goons patrolling the outside of the circle. "We don't need the wolves to distract the coven inside the circle. All we need is for them to distract those guards on the outside."

"We can do that," Kevin said. "But what's the point?"

"Give us a couple minutes head start, then keep their attention focused on you for as long as you can."

"What are you going to do?"

"We're out of time. I've got to find a way to get inside that circle. We've got to do this now."

I turned my back on them and started picking my way through the headstones as quickly as I could. Rhys was right beside me. There was a pretty good path between the headstones that we could follow around the hill to the back of the tree. If we kept low and quiet, the guards wouldn't see us, and the torches inside the circle would keep the cultists from seeing us until it was too late.

I hoped.

We were less than a dozen steps from the tree when I heard the signal—a long, haunting howl that was immediately picked up and echoed by a quartet of answering howls, from all around us. Their song raised goose bumps up my arms.

CHAPTER 18

WOLVES RACED TOWARD the circle from the surrounding hills. Silent, streaking shadows moving so swiftly, they seemed an inky cloud spreading across the starlit landscape. And there were a lot more than five. At least fifty or more. Answering howls, hidden from view, echoed across the cemetery, their message clear—*we're coming*.

Rhys and I had reached the outer edge of the circle—hidden from the coven by the massive trunk of the spirit tree. I chanced a quick peek around the edge to judge the coven's reaction.

Nothing in their demeanor indicated that they were even aware of the wolves or Rhys and I. On the opposite side of the summoning circle, the three guards had seen the pack moving in. They stood side-by-side, facing the pack, their stun batons at the ready. Good. The distraction should give Rhys and me a chance.

I had my shears out, and Rhys had drawn his sword. He pounded and stabbed at the invisible shield, to no effect. I tried the same with my shears, but the barrier surrounding the summoning circle was a thick, invisible wall of air—like rubber cement.

A muffled scream of terror from inside the summoning circle caught my attention. Honey was awake. Bound as she was, she'd managed to wriggle off the altar and lay helpless in the grass. Baldy grabbed her by the arm, the knife in his other hand glittering in the torchlight. John Fewkes never stopped his chanting, but nodded at Baldy to put her back on the altar.

Baldy lifted Honey by one arm and flung her, like a ragdoll, onto the granite slab of the altar. She squirmed to a kneeling position, but with both her hands and feet bound, she could hardly move.

He grabbed her and she spit at him. He retaliated with a punch to her face.

Her head whipped back—the force of his blow knocked her sprawling across the altar, blood streaming from her nose and lips. Baldy held her down, the sharp blade at her throat, his eyes turned to Fewkes as if waiting for a signal. Blood dripped steadily from her broken nose, pooling on the altar. Silvery threads reached out from the spirit tree, like tendrils of seeking roots, questing blindly toward the bloody altar.

My chest tightened. "What the hell is that?" They were so close, but we couldn't get to them. I wanted to tear my hair out.

"It's too early for blood," Rhys said. "That's not right."

Liddy moved to the altar where Lou lay, holding her knife less than an inch from his right eye.

Arby lay unconscious on the center altar, blessedly unaware of the murderous drama around him. In another minute or two, it would all be over.

I had to act now. I willed my shears into my hand and leapt toward the summoning circle. Rhys and I hit the wall together and collided with an invisible shield as firm as a rubber ball. We both staggered back and I fell. I scrambled to my feet.

I slammed my arm against the force field repeatedly with the same results. I kicked at it, and even tried stabbing at it with my shears, but it made no difference. A dozen feet from me, Rhys paced warily, his efforts no better than mine.

Nothing made any difference.

Inside the circle, the tendrils from the spirit tree

had grown thicker. The chanting had stopped. Liddy and the other cultists stood at rigid attention, waiting instructions from their leader, the black sorcerer, John Fewkes. The press of power gathering within the circle increased, approaching critical mass, like an overinflated tire getting ready to blow. Then, at a nod from Fewkes, Baldy plunged, his knife into Honey's chest.

Noooo!

The spirit tree's tendrils crept like a carpet toward each of the altars, moving fastest toward the dark stain spreading out across Honey's pale blue tee shirt.

I fell to my knees, cursing. I pressed my hands up against the unyielding, greasy shield of the summoning circle. The keening wail of the wolves grew louder, echoing across the vale.

Rhys panted beside me, breathing hard, as if he'd run a long ways.

"We're too late," I told him. I could barely speak—my breath came in shuddering gasps. *Too late, too late, too late...*

"Don't," Rhys said, with a certainty that came from a millennia of experience. His anger brought me back to myself. "We're not done yet. Think."

"I'm trying!"

Thready roots, leading from the tree to the altar

180

where Honey lay in a pool of her own blood, thickened and twisted together into corded cables of what looked like pale grey ectoplasm. Blindly, the rootlets sought the red liquid, and on contact, blackened and thickened as the blood was siphoned up and flowed back to the tree.

Rhys tried using his short sword as a shovel to cut a path beneath the surface of the soil, but the circle seemed to extend into the earth as well.

Liddy moved in on Lou, like a tigress stalking her prey, but he was ready for her. Even with one leg encased in a thick cast, he managed to land a solid kick with his other foot, hitting Liddy square in the chest. She fell and dropped the knife. The rootlets reached for it, and began to cover the blade. Liddy had to wrest it away.

The first drops of Honey's blood reached the spirit tree, and the trunk began to twist, emitting a series of sharp cracking sounds. Dust and needles rained down on us in torrents. Thousands more rootlets reached for Honey's chest, covering it. Baldy stared in mute fascination.

"Quit screwing around, Mattie—just do it!" Rhys ordered. He panted like an angry dog, his sweatshirt wet with sweat. He looked as angry and dispirited as I felt. He stalked the edge of the circle like an angry panther.

The immense tree began to jerk, as if a great moth was about to emerge from its cocoon.

CHAPTER 19

THE FIRST PALE roots of the spirit tree reached the altars where Lou and Arby lay, slithering between the row of black-eyed dolls surrounding the unconscious boy. One of those dolls had begged Morta to for help. That had been weeks ago. I should have listened.

I cursed the decision we'd made to keep Charlie out of this. He could have freed the trapped souls inside those dolls. Without the dozen souls, the ceremony would certainly fail. But Charlie was too old and fragile—he wasn't up to something like this. It had only been a few months since I'd ripped a hole in his soul when I'd incorrectly banished his djemon.

A sudden idea came to me. "Oh!" Of course the words of the incantation were right there—I had to remind myself to be careful every time I banished a djemon. I knew the words by heart. This I knew I could do.

"Get ready," I said.

Rhys glared at me, his short sword in one hand, Morta's two-foot long Kinjali dagger in the other. "Do it!"

Liddy Fewkes made another tentative stab at Lou, who he managed to dodge by rolling off the edge of the altar.

I took a deep breath and yelled. "Zeypax! I summon you!"

A ghostly shadow hovered in the air before me. I couldn't see Zeypax, exactly, but I could sense his pissed-off presence. When I'd banished him, it was only from materializing physically in any earthly plane. I'd rendered him incapable of answering to or serving his master, but he was still attached to his master's soul. Even after his master's death, he would only be able to exist in the ether. I wasn't in physical contact with the sorcerer, but I didn't need to be. I was stronger now. I reached for Morta's light and let it fill me.

The crown of the spirit tree began to whip back and forth, filling the air with needles and dust. Something was fighting its way out of the top of that tree.

"I hereby banish Zeypax, the djemon servant

184

of John Fewkes, *from every and all* physical and metaphysical planes, never to return!"

From inside the summoning circle, the sorcerer let out a scream of agony and grabbed his chest. His knees crumpled and he fell to the ground.

With a soft pop, the protective wards around the summoning circle disappeared.

CHAPTER 20

A DOZEN SNARLING wolves dashed forward and encircled the coven, herding them like sheep into a tight cluster. At Fewkes' collapse, Baldy and Liddy had rushed to his side. Baldy was the first to realize that the shield surrounding the summoning circle was gone. He picked up the knife that John had dropped and stormed toward us.

"I've got this," Rhys said to me. Get the boy."

John Fewkes lay on the ground in a fetal position, between me and Arby, his expression a painful grimace. Zeypax had been a good-sized demon—probably served his master for decades before I came along. Banishing Zeypax must've hurt like hell. The sorcerer clutched his chest, fighting for breath. Good.

The top of the ancient yew whipped around like a sapling, broken branches and needles rained down upon the clearing. The sounds of wood cracking and the blade-on-blade battle between Rhys and Baldy filled the air.

I swept the wooden dolls off the altar and gathered Arby's limp body into my arms, feeling for a pulse at his neck. *There*. My shears made short work of the zip ties that had been used to bind his hands and feet. What kind of cowards would do such a thing to a child?

Something grabbed at my ankle. Instinctively, I kicked out, knocking Fewkes' hand away.

From behind me, a familiar voice said, "Give me the boy."

I whirled, clutching Arby tightly to me.

Liddy Fewkes held a sacrificial knife in her blood-covered hands. Her expression held no fear—only a flinty determination. She held the blade with a casual familiarity that made me believe she knew how to use it. I glanced at the bloody third altar, where Lou had been lying, but he was no longer visible. Grey-white rootlets stretched from the spirit tree to the stone altar.

Shit. I held my shears in front of me. "Stay back," I ordered.

Off to my left, I heard a sudden curse from Rhys and a shout from Baldy was abruptly cut off. In the distance, sounds of an approaching helicopter echoed across the vale. A searchlight honed in on the frantic movement of the treetop.

From the center of the trunk, a sharp crack rang out, and the tree sort of exploded outward, directly toward us, spraying us with splinters and pointed shards. The concussion threw us back a dozen feet.

A ragged crevice opened up at the root line of the tree, and ran up the trunk. The bark of the giant yew peeled back from the central core, branches and all. A rich evergreen scent filled the air. Black, opaque smoke drifted up and out of the exposed inner bark. It quickly coalesced onto a long, narrow figure, some twelve feet high, with glowing red eyes. Will-o-the-wisps encircled it like a manic halo.

At the explosion, Liddy had ducked behind the altar, but she was back, coming toward me with knife in hand.

I backed away. From somewhere behind me, one of the cultists screamed.

Overhead, the black smoke compressed and the figure gained substance as it grew. A mouth opened. I was close enough to see several rows of pale pointed teeth emerge from blackened gums. Its fetid breath filled the air with the reek of burning pitch. My eyes watered. I coughed to clear my throat and lungs.

The helicopter flew closer. I recognized the logo of a local television station. The Nalusa Falaya pawed at the searchlight, as if the glare hurt its eyes, but when whoever was manning the light didn't get the hint, the demon stretched its long arms out thinner and thinner to grab at the chopper with its long skinny claws.

The pilot only narrowly avoided contact, and immediately backed off. The searchlight went out.

In the flickering torchlight, Rhys was on his feet—running at the demon full tilt, the gleaming blade of his long sword angled for a killing blow. He hit the creature with a mighty swing, and the blade bit deep into the black flesh. There was a spark where the blade met flesh and the demon screamed. The earth shook. I felt my eardrums pop and warm blood tickled down my jaw. I scrambled to my feet and ran toward them, screaming his name at the top of my lungs.

The Nalusa Falaya scooped up Rhys and shook him until his sword went flying. After a moment's inspection, the demon bared a toothsome grin and threw Rhys at the gaping crevasse in the center of the spirit tree. The impact shook the whole tree, and another shower of dust, branches, and needles rained down upon the scene.

Rhys grunted. A spar, thick as a broom handle protruded from his shoulder. He hung, suspended in the heart of the tree, until he caught sight of me running toward him, cradling Arby in my arms.

But the Nalusa Falaya wasn't finished. He gripped the spirit tree by the trunk and with little apparent effort, twisted the yew's trunk until the crevice disappeared, sealing Rhys inside. The tree appeared whole again. The pale rootlets, which had emerged from the tree, broke off during the demon's efforts, and lay like crispy noodles, scattered around the base of the tree.

"Rhys!"

He was trapped inside the spirit tree as surely as a djenie in a bottle. I dropped Arby and raced toward the demon, my shears aloft to strike, the beat of angry drums and Morta's magic thrumming in my veins. "I hereby banish--."

The monster batted me aside like a bothersome gnat. I flew a dozen yards before crashing against one of the larger tombstones, the breath knocked out of me. I gasped for air, fighting to remain conscious. Pain—serious pain, spasmed through me like a full-body cramp.

This couldn't be happening. The Nalusa Falaya was free. How the hell had everything gone to shit so fast?

Liddy Fewkes walked unsteadily toward the tall black figure. "I greet you, Nalusa Falaya. You have been freed as promised," she said. Her voice trembled, but she stood firm. "Fulfill your part of our bargain and grant me the immortality you swore to deliver on your release."

The creature scanned the carnage of bloody and broken bodies within the circle. "My oath was to your brother," it said, its voice like the crunch of boots on gravel. "I see him not."

She pointed to the huddled form of John Fewkes, who lay where he had fallen, amid the clutter of scattered dolls and carved figures. "It is too late for him. Take the sacrifices offered and fulfill your vow to me."

The Nalusa Falaya leaned down and poked at the sorcerer's body with a six-inch claw. Fewkes groaned. The monster nodded. Then, casually, as if picking up a canapé it plucked up one of the wooden dolls and popped it into its mouth. Its eyes widened, seemingly in appreciation, and glowed red like a pair of giant rubies. It proceeded to consume the remaining wooden figures with single-minded concentration; one-by-one, in rapid succession, until all were gone. Each time it shoved one of the spirit-trapped offerings into its maw, it seemed to solidify and grow even taller, until it towered above the scene like some giant black cobra with long skinny arms and claws.

Something was terribly wrong with me. I could not move. I wondered if my back was broken. Arby lay unconscious in the grass, out of reach, oblivious to everything. I thought if I could speak, maybe I could banish it, but I couldn't get enough breath to get the words out.

The demon gave Liddy a sly look. "I shall fulfill my vow as soon as you are ready."

Smiling, Liddy took a deep breath, as if to brace herself for what was to come. "You may proceed."

In less than an eye-blink, the demon snatched her up and bit off her head.

From somewhere behind me, I heard the collective gasp from the cultists. A wolf whined nearby.

The Nalusa Falaya threw his head back and tossed the rest of her body down his throat, like a snake swallowing prey. It licked the blood from its lips and with surprising care, assisted an ashen-faced John Fewkes into a sitting position. Fewkes appeared not at all cowed by the presence of the demon.

In spite of my pain, a little thrill of satisfaction raced through me—I'd hurt him badly. Fewkes was mortal—by destroying Zeypax, I'd torn that hole in his soul—maybe even big enough to kill him.

The creature addressed John Fewkes. "Three things were required of you in exchange for my gift: an equal number of souls as was used to imprison me, an immortal to take my place inside the tree, and the sacrifice of your dearest love. The number of spirits offered was correct. When I escaped the tree, I did not detect the presence of your demon Zeypax, but the djenie warrior was an acceptable replacement. The blood of your sister as sacrifice revived me and I am whole again as I was before." The Nalusa Falaya bowed deeply. "I am in your debt, sorcerer. Are you ready for your gift?"

On the crest of the hill above us, flashlights beams cast eerie shadows through the trees. If that was the Sheriff and his men, they were too late. The wolves surrounding the cultists began to pace nervously. I tried to call out, but it was no use. I couldn't even wave my arms.

Fewkes sat up straighter. "Just to be clear. I will be immortal, with access to all the same knowledge and magic you yourself possess. I shall neither die, nor age, nor suffer any infirmities."

The demon nodded its head in acquiescence. "As you say, so it shall be."

There was a shout from the top of the hill. Too dark to see who, but from the number of flashlights, I guessed six or seven men at least. It didn't matter. It was too late.

"Fulfill your end of our bargain," Fewkes said.

The Nalusa Falaya dissolved itself into a transparent black smoke. It whirled itself into a long whiplike shape, and dove straight into John Fewkes chest.

Holy shit.

It took several long moments before the Nalusa Falaya disappeared completely into the sorcerer's body. The high priest coughed and spat, then coughed again. He scrambled to his feet, shook himself like a wet dog, and leapt up onto the center altar with surprising ease.

Several of the cultists shouted out to him, alerting him of the approach of law enforcement. Fewkes ignored them, spread his arms wide, and turned in a slow circle, stopping only when he saw me.

From less than twenty feet away, I got a good look at the changes in his appearance. Same face, but leaner. Harder. The pot belly was gone. His eyes reflected red in the torchlight.

Good God, what have I done? The sudden realization of my grievous mistake slammed home like a bolt of lightning. Banishing Zeypax hadn't stopped the summoning; it had opened the door for the demon. Tearing that hole in the sorcerer's soul had provided the anchor the Nalusa Falaya needed in order to grant John Fewkes the powers and immortality he craved. Like Annie had moved into Charlie's broken soul, so too, the Nalusa Falaya had moved into the soul of John Fewkes.

Someone fired a warning shot and the wolves streaked away into the forest. A voice, magnified through a bullhorn, said "Drop your weapons and freeze! Armed Federal officers with warrants."

The men had reached the edge of the summoning circle. I recognized Ted Roper immediately. His expression went from one of wary alertness to shock as he took in the scene. Dimly, I wondered how many bodies they'd find.

"Thank you, Miss Blackman," John Fewkes said. "I admit I had my doubts that this would work at all. Without the Hand of Fate, I fear that freeing the Nalusa Falaya would not have been possible. I must be going now, but rest assured, you'll be hearing from me soon." He laughed, loud and long. Then, with a dramatic swish of his hand, he transformed into a raven the size of a Labrador retriever.

The officers froze, guns drawn, their faces agape.

The raven-Fewkes thing cackled and flapped his wings, then launched himself from the altar into the night.

Several of the officers fired shots, but the agent in charge ordered them to hold their fire.

In the sudden silence, everyone turned to look at me.

CHAPTER 21

I WOKE UP in the hospital cuffed to the bed by my ankle. Even without the cuff, I could hardly move. One arm was taped to a protective brace surrounding my rib cage. The doctor said I'd sustained a concussion, broken ribs, bruised lungs, a broken collarbone, and three spinal fractures. Not that it mattered. He also said that the feds wanted to talk to me.

That afternoon, I was interviewed by Agent Nelson Hardesty, the head of the FBI field unit office in Rochester, and Hughie Green, one of the Bureau's top supernatural investigators, from Quantico. Sheriff Reynolds was there, but he didn't look too happy about it. This wasn't his show. Green conducted the interview.

Green was a big guy, probably pushing six-foot

six and maybe two-thirty, while Hardesty was one of those pasty-faced administrator-types with a military haircut, steel-rimmed glasses and a permanently pissy expression.

"Is Arby okay?" I asked. I was on oxygen, but it was hard to get a breath.

"Mrs. Briscoe is expected to recover. Her son is still in a coma, his prognosis is unknown."

"They're alive?" I blinked back tears of relief. I looked at Reynolds. "What about Lou?"

Reynolds shook his head. So Lou was dead, then. My friend, my fault. I should have done more, been more, seen more. I should have been smarter.

Green and Hardesty exchanged a look. "We still don't have a clear picture of exactly what happened." Green's voice held a pleasant rumble. Sure, he was playing 'good cop', but I liked him. And unlike agent Roper, or his predecessor, Frank Porter, I sensed that Green had more than good looks and athleticism going for him. His lifeline gave off the same kind of intense glow as the crescent scar on my hand and the coin Lou had given me.

"Am I under arrest?"

Hardesty said "Maybe" at the same time Green said "Not at the moment."

No point in asking for a lawyer. No point in lying

to them. The agents had been there. They'd seen what happened for themselves—at least the last part of it. And of course they'd been right there when John Fewkes had thanked me for helping him free the Nalusa Falaya. They just didn't believe what they'd seen.

At least the werewolves were safe—I'd seen the pack take off as soon as the officers cleared the trees. So that meant the only witnesses they had were Honey, the surviving cultists, and Rhys--*oh god, Rhys, I'm so sorry*.

A wave of nausea washed though me. Rhys was gone. The way he'd looked for me in that final moment, and how I'd felt when his eyes reached mine. I'd seen his soul in that final glimpse of him. His hopes and dreams turned to ash, all because of me. I blinked back sudden tears. He'd told me once that the only thing a djenie feared, the worst fate imaginable, was being imprisoned. The human idea of the genie in a lamp was every djenie's worst nightmare. He'd trusted me with his death, he said, and instead I'd delivered him to a fate far worse than death. He'd offered me his heart and I'd pushed him away. I closed my eyes and swallowed the lump in my throat. My fault.

Lou was gone. Honey and Arby's lives had just been destroyed by what they'd endured. And it wasn't over.

Fewkes was immortal now, and he had the Nalusa Falaya with him. People would start dying soon.

I sighed. Life as I knew it was over. "I'll tell you whatever you want to know."

And so I told them.

About the stakeout with Lou and discovering the graveyard and the coven and the layering ritual we'd seen. About getting spotted and Lou's warning about the Penfield witch cult.

About Lou's getting run down by the limo and going to the Sheriff and the FBI with my suspicions about the Penfield witch cult and getting the brush off. And as I told them that part, I got mad again.

I got even madder when I told them about Lou and Honey's warnings about the Fewkes being sorcerers and deciding on my own to check out the Fewkes's store and realizing that I'd made a huge mistake by going inside because John Fewkes scared the living crap out of me.

And I got madder still, when it dawned on me that I nothing I said could undo what John Fewkes had done. Nate was dead. So was Honey's grandmother. And Lou—how many others had died at the hands of that sorcerer and his cult? How many souls had he trapped and held to feed the Nalusa Falaya? There were now two immortal monsters running loose the world, and that thought totally pissed me off. In my head, the sound of drums throbbed a backbeat to the angry thrum of my pulse.

So I told them the simple truth—the only thing that would make the FBI sit up and take notice.

I told them that John Fewkes was a demon master. To the biggest baddest, most evil immortal creature imaginable.

The FBI had no idea what they were dealing with. Oh they'd make all the right noises, and beg the government for more funds, but I had no doubt that it would take the FBI a very long time to realize that you can't kill an immortal.

I didn't mention the werewolves, the Penfield Eight, or the trapped spirits. No need to drag Charlie or Honey or Kevin or the werewolves or anyone else any deeper into this mess.

And I never said a word about Rhys.

He and Lou were both gone. My mistake, and one that I would spend the rest of my life trying to correct. And something the demon said to Fewkes had given me an idea. If the Nalusa Falaya had been captured once, it could be captured again. I had no idea how to do it, but nothing—neither the living nor the dead— would stop me.

Three hours later, after the agents were satisfied

I'd told them everything they wanted to know, Hardesty unlocked the cuff from my ankle, saying it had just been a precaution, and thanked me for my cooperation. Hughie Green gave me his card and said to call him if I remembered anything else.

Sheriff Reynolds winked at me. I'd just lied through my teeth to the FBI and he knew it.

Yeah. Reynolds likes me.

Here in Shore Haven, we take care of our own. John Fewkes would regret the day he ever set foot in Shore Haven. This was war.

END

ABOUT THE AUTHOR

Award-winning author Sharon Joss writes science fiction, fantasy and horror. She is the author of seven novels, including *Aurum*, *Brothers of the Fang*, and the alternate history thriller, *Steam Dogs*. In 2015, she won the Writers of the Future Golden Pen award for speculative fiction with her novella, *Stars That Make Dark Heaven Light*. She lives in Oregon and writes full-time. Find out more about her and her books by going to www.sharonjoss.com

AUTHOR'S NOTE

Thank you for giving this book a read. If you enjoyed it, please tell your friends and consider leaving a review on Amazon or Goodreads, even if it's only a line or two; it would make all the difference and would be very much appreciated. If you'd like a quick note when I have a new release, please sign up for my new release mailing list at:

http://bit.ly/1UkJZTa

Your email will never be shared and you can unsubscribe at any time. I'll send you a free e-book right away and occasionally send out information about contests or opportunities to snag review copies).

MORE GREAT TITLES FROM SHARON JOSSA

DETECTIVE MIKE BANE is a shape shifter with two beasts: a 300-lb black jaguar with a taste for turtle meat, and a psychotic Olmec shaman named Tehuantl with a taste for blood.

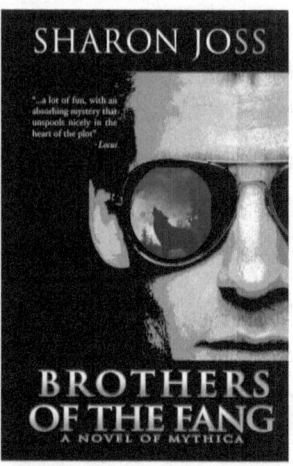

When Mike accepts a security job at Mythica, America's only supernatural theme park, he discovers an unexpected kinship with the park's werewolf pack. But when his curiosity gets the best of him, he's ensnared in a centuries-old feud between Mythica's vampires and the fae of the neighboring High Tor clan. Only Tehuantl's magic can save Mike's brothers of the fang; in return, Tehuantl wants permanent possession of Mike's body, mind, and soul.

A DANGEROUS ADVENTURE, A BEAUTIFUL WOMAN, AND GOLD

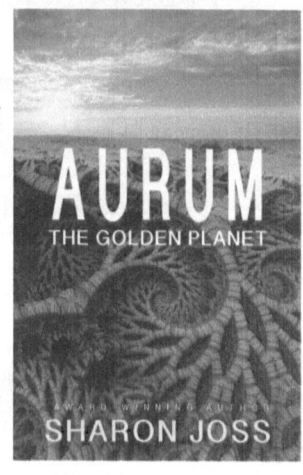

AURUM is a story of survival and perseverance in the face of extinction as master engraver Renly Harkness and the beautiful half-breed, K'Sati, embark on an exploration deep into the forbidden zone of this plague planet. With their own lives on the line and time slipping away, Renly and K'Sati battle greedy human predators, aliens, and a myriad of genetic viruses.

MORE GREAT TITLES FROM SHARON JOSS

In this alternate history thriller, 19th-century technology and the supernatural collide outside London, when airships and aerialists from across Europe converge on the Isle of Dogs for an air show. Among the crowd, Simon Atters, a master thief with his eye on the Queen's jewels, a Metropolitan Police inspector, and a former royal wizard with supernatural powers who is dead set on kidnapping the commander of the most powerful army in the world—Queen Victoria of Britain.

Winner of the
2015 GOLDEN PEN AWARD

Worlds and species collide on the planet Hesperidee in this classic winning tale of love, duty, and the future of humanity.

"STARS THAT MAKE DARK HEAVEN LIGHT is an amazing story, as powerful as it is beautiful. Award-winning author Sharon Joss manages to prove herself to be one of the best writers of our time."
--New York Times bestselling author
David Farland

Look for the next volume in the Hand of Fate series:

COMING SOON